"Heart-wrenching and heartwarming, Rachel's story forced me out of my comfort zone and gave me a picture of what practical compassion looks like for a Christian. I highly recommend it!"

—ERYNN MANGUM,
author of the LAUREN HOLBROOK series and the MAYA DAVIS series

DECEIVED

LURED FROM THE TRUTH

Melody Carlson

TH1NK, an
Imprint of
NavPress

NAVPRESS

Discipleship Inside Out®

NavPress is the publishing ministry of The Navigators, an international Christian organization and leader in personal spiritual development. NavPress is committed to helping people grow spiritually and enjoy lives of meaning and hope through personal and group resources that are biblically rooted, culturally relevant, and highly practical.

For a free catalog go to www.NavPress.com
or call 1.800.366.7788 in the United States or 1.800.839.4769 in Canada.

© 2012 by Melody Carlson

ISBN-13: 978-1-60006-952-9

Cover image by VanHart/Shutterstock Images LLC

Published in association with the literary agency of Sara A. Fortenberry

Some of the anecdotal illustrations in this book are true to life and are included with the permission of the persons involved. All other illustrations are composites of real situations, and any resemblance to people living or dead is coincidental.

Unless otherwise identified, all Scripture quotations in this publication are taken from the *Holy Bible, New International Version*® (NIV®). Copyright © 1973, 1978, 1984, 2011 by Biblica. Used by permission of Zondervan. All rights reserved.

Carlson, Melody.
  Deceived : lured from the truth / Melody Carlson.
    pages cm -- (Secrets ; [bk. 5])
  Summary: "Lured by the possibility of a relationship with a boy she likes, Rachel secretly attends his cult-like church. Slowly but surely, she is lured into a religion that goes against everything she's ever been taught"-- Provided by publisher.
  ISBN 978-1-60006-952-9
  [1. Cults--Fiction. 2. Christian life--Fiction.] I. Title.
  PZ7.C216637De 2012
  [Fic]--dc23
                                    2012022457

Printed in the United States of America

1 2 3 4 5 6 7 8 / 16 15 14 13 12

Nothing in my life has prepared me for this. And I don't mean spending my summer sweltering behind the counter of Nadine's Natural Ice Cream Parlor either. I can handle scooping out sticky, drippy ice cream orders. And I know how to be polite to entitled rich kids — even the ones with zero manners. The personal disillusionment I'm referring to is the sad realization that I am now the product of a broken home. Yes, I know the term *broken home* is hopelessly old-fashioned. But so am I.

"It's official," my mom called to tell me at seven thirty this morning. "The papers came through, and as of midnight last night, your father and I are legally divorced."

"I'm sorry, Mom." I sat up in bed, blinking into the bright July sunlight streaming through the dusty window next to my bunk and trying to remember where I was . . . and *why*. Oh, yes, the women's dormitory at Rock Canyon Lake Resort, a bare-bones barracks where summer workers are housed together like sardines . . . or inmates. I'll admit I was thrilled to come here at first. I imagined myself working in one of the swanky restaurants, improving my culinary-art skills. Instead I'm peddling ice cream.

"I'm sorry too," Mom said a bit too cheerily. "But I'm also greatly relieved. At least it's finally over. I can get on with *my* life now."

I bit my tongue, knowing that getting on with *her* life was just another way of saying she was ready to start dating again. Although the truth is, she has already begun dating—on the sly since she knows how much I disapprove. But now that her marriage is legally "dissolved" and I'm living up here for the summer, I know she feels completely free to do whatever she wants with whomever she likes.

It's futile for me to point out that divorce or no divorce, she and my dad are still breaking a sacred vow they made to God. I've watched their wedding video enough times to know that they got married in the church and promised to love each other and stay together "in sickness and in health" and "for richer or poorer" and so on and so forth until death forced them to part ways.

However, not even twenty years later and they're still both very much alive . . . and according to Mom, they're "legally" parted. And I could tell by her voice, she's happy about it. In fact, I'll bet she's already planning a big date tonight to celebrate her newfound freedom.

After I grab my towel and shower bag, shuffling off toward the bathroom, I wonder if that wasn't the real reason she farmed me off with her friend Nadine for the summer. "Just think of the money you can make for culinary school," she told me as she drove me up here three weeks ago. "And living with a bunch of young people in the dorm—well, it'll be so fun for you. I'm already starting to get jealous. Seriously, Rachel, with the lake right there and all the beautiful scenery, it's like being on a paid vacation."

Vacation-smacation. It was just her convenient way to get rid of me for a while.

I get in the shower line and estimate how long it will be until my turn. Not that I'm in any particular hurry since I'm up earlier than usual, but hopefully there'll still be hot water.

"Mind if I take cuts?" a short blonde named Steffie asks me hopefully. "I have to be at the Blue Moose by nine and your ice cream parlor doesn't open until later, right?"

I shrug. "Go ahead." I don't point out that although Nadine's doesn't open until eleven, I still have to be there at nine thirty to get the place ready to go, which means getting a head start on making waffle cones and receiving deliveries. Plus I try to air out the stuffy shop in the morning while it's still cool, and I get everything cleaned up better than it was left the night before.

I also don't point out to Steffie that the ice cream parlor is one of the hottest, stickiest places to work in the resort, thanks to the recent high temps. Washing dishes at the Blue Moose Café might be worse, although I doubt that's Steffie's job. I also doubt she'd care to hear me whining about Nadine's. Everyone around here seems pretty self-absorbed. Their problems are major; mine are invisible.

No one cares that Nadine's broken-down AC isn't scheduled to be fixed anytime soon. Or that despite the two box fans Nadine dropped off on Tuesday, the lack of AC combined with the heat produced by the refrigeration units makes the ice cream parlor nearly uninhabitable.

But does that keep people from coming in there for their mocha fudge delight sundaes or their triple-berry yogurt smoothies? Think again. And when they have to wait very long, which is often the case, they get pretty impatient and grumpy.

All they want is to grab their cool treats and escape the sweltering little sweatshop. Really, who can blame them?

A couple more girls entice me to give them cuts in the shower line before I finally put my foot down, which doesn't endear me to anyone. Not that I particularly care as I jump into a shower that's quickly turning lukewarm. I hurry to rub a special keratin conditioner into my hair before the spray turns icy cold. And I try not to listen to Steffie and another girl exchanging stories about their previous evening.

Shortly after arriving here several weeks ago, I learned that this is a party crowd. And if you go along with them — partying, I mean — they'll all act like your very best friends. But if you stand up for your own personal convictions, like I attempted to do right from the start, they pretty much freeze you out. Kind of like the water is starting to do right now. I hear some warning yelps from other bathers, and just as I'm rinsing conditioner out of my long hair, I get my ice-cold wake-up call too. But I don't scream like the others. What's the point?

I turn off the water and grab my towel. Ignoring the snide comments from some of the restaurant girls still waiting in line — girls who should've partied less and gotten up earlier — I hurry back to my bunk to get dressed in the silly pink-and-white-striped uniform of camp shirt and shorty-shorts Nadine thinks is "just adorable." Someone should make her wear it. However, being that Nadine is the boss and owner and pushing fifty, I doubt that's going to happen anytime soon.

And to be fair, Nadine is actually pretty nice. I appreciate how she trusts me enough to give me some managerial responsibilities including allowing me to open for her. Plus she pays me a fair wage. No, this isn't about Nadine. It's just that I'm in a foul mood today.

As I walk through the immaculately clean resort (Nadine told me they have a sanitation crew that goes through in the wee hours of the morning to ensure it's "tidier than Disneyland"), I try to rally my spirits. When I first arrived at Rock Canyon Lake Resort, I was somewhat charmed by its well-maintained and old-fashioned decor. It was created to resemble an old west town with false-front buildings and boardwalks and old-fashioned businesses like Maybelle's Mercantile or the Sarsaparilla Saloon, and it seemed like a great place to bring a family.

My first reaction was to assume that this resort was just my cup of tea. Kind of like going back in time, or so I imagined. I don't like to admit to most people that I consider myself to be an old-fashioned girl, but I sometimes confide to close friends that I feel like I was born in the wrong era, that I would've fit in much better if I'd been born into my grandparents' genera- tion — they were teens in the late fifties. I even have Grandma Lindy's old poodle skirt and oxfords to prove it.

But the problem with this resort is that the charm is skin deep. It only took a week to figure out that most of the people who stay here are wealthy, entitled, selfish, and impatient. They treat me like I'm less than them — or worse, like I'm invisible or have no feelings. And they almost never tip.

However, as I unlock the door to Nadine's, I am suddenly encouraged by an unexpected thought. *Today is Thursday*. And although it's not the end of my workweek, it does mean there'll be an LSD delivery today. Okay, I'll admit the first time Nadine said that to me, I nearly fell over. Was she really expecting a delivery of illegal drugs? But she quickly explained that LSD stands for Lost Springs Dairy and they deliver on Monday and Thursday mornings around ten thirty.

Lost Springs Dairy is Nadine's main provider of the locally

made all-natural organic ice cream. And it's not that I'm over the moon for their ice cream, although it's pretty yummy. It's simply that the guy who makes these deliveries, a certain Josiah Davis, is totally yummy. Okay, *yummy* is the wrong word. He's just plain old handsome. But perhaps even more impressive than his looks is that he seems to be genuinely nice. And in a place like this where people can be cruel, someone as thoughtful and kind as Josiah is most welcome. And it doesn't hurt that he has this amazing Australian accent.

Of course, as soon as I'm inside of Nadine's, I realize that considering it's Thursday, I should've taken more care with my appearance this morning. Not only did I walk out without even peeking into a mirror, but I didn't bother to dry my hair. So in the midst of giving the tiny employee restroom a quick wipe down, I take a couple minutes to dig some mascara and lip gloss from my purse.

I know I'm lucky to have good skin — I've had like three zits in my entire life — so my beauty routine is pretty low maintenance. My friend Carlie complains about this all the time.

"You're just naturally beautiful," she tells me about once a week. Then she'll offer to trade her pale, freckled face for my smooth dark bronze skin. And without hurting her feelings, I always remind her that we should be thankful for the way God made us.

As I comb my long, dark hair back into a smooth ponytail, I'm relieved I took time to condition it. The keratin straightening treatment is supposed to last all summer if I take care of it. Now that I've primped a bit, I start to put on the silly polka-dot apron that's part of my uniform, then stop myself. Since the shop's not officially open, I can postpone that bit of humiliation until after Josiah's delivery.

I've just finished cleaning the front window and door when I see the blue-and-white LSD truck coming down the street. I peer out, trying to make sure Josiah's driving today, but the truck whips down a side street before I can see. However, when I go to the rear of the store, quickly rinsing the vinegar glass cleaner from my hands and unlocking the back door, I spy the truck pulling into the alley and am pleased to see Josiah waving from the driver's seat.

Grinning like a goofball, I eagerly wave back. It seems impossible that I'm this glad to see someone I've met only a few times before. But it's like he's my long-lost best friend . . . or even something more. "Hey, Josiah," I call as he hops out of the van.

"Good *die*, Rachel Hebert," he says with an accent that melts me even faster than a dropped scoop on a July afternoon. "How's my favorite sheila doing?"

By now I know *sheila* is Australian slang, kind of like *chick*. "Just fine. How are you?"

"Couldn't be better." He grins as he opens up the back of the truck, emerging with a wooden crate in his hands. "But it's going to be a hot one, I hear."

I nod as I hold the door open for him. "Triple digits again."

He looks puzzled as he sets the crate on the back counter. *"Triple digits?"*

Now I realize we have a language barrier. "I mean, the temperature is going to be more than a hundred degrees."

He looks shocked. "A *hundred* degrees?"

"That's what I heard someone say . . ."

"Oh yeah." He pushes a strand of dark hair away from his forehead and smiles directly into my eyes. "You mean *Yankee* degrees."

"Huh?"

"Yanks use Fahrenheit, which seems unnecessarily confusing to an Aussie. Why not just use Celsius? It's so much simpler."

"Right." I nod as I remember what I learned in chemistry. "Fahrenheit and Celsius degrees are different, aren't they? I just can't recall exactly how it works at the moment." How can I be expected to remember science when I'm looking into those intense brown eyes framed in dark brown brows?

"Zero degrees Celsius means it's freezing," he explains patiently. "I reckon that's about thirty degrees Fahrenheit or thereabouts." Now his forehead creases as if he's calculating something. "So one hundred degrees for you would be about forty Celsius for us." He laughs. "But one hundred degrees Celsius is hot enough to boil water. If it were that hot today, we'd all be toast."

I laugh too as I follow him back out for another crate. "Well, it gets pretty hot in here. I'll probably feel like toast by the end of my day."

"At least you can go jump in the lake." He sets the second crate on the counter.

"I suppose . . ." I glance out the window. How hot would I have to be to run out there and jump in the lake all by myself? It would be one thing if I had friends to do it with.

"You seem sad, Rachel." He leans over and peers curiously into my eyes. "Something bothering you?"

Surprised by his unexpected kindness, a lump lodges in my throat. But not wanting to break down in front of this cool guy, I quickly look away. "I'm okay," I say in a gruff voice.

"Out with it," he urges. Then he places his hand on my forearm and turns me around to face him. "I can tell something's not right. What's troubling you?"

I look into his face, which looks honestly concerned, and despite my resolve to be strong, tears fill my eyes. Then I'm telling him about my mom's wake-up call. "And she announces that my parents' marriage is over as of today." I sigh. "It's completely dissolved. Just like that."

"I'm sorry. That's really rough."

I nod as I reach for an organic napkin. "I mean, I realize that lots of people go through this." I wipe my nose with rough paper. "It's just that I never thought it would happen to *my* family. I mean, we were so normal. I thought we were happy. And we always went to church together and—and—" My voice cracks with emotion, and I realize this is way too much information to share with someone I hope to get to know better.

Just mentioning my church is like opening a fresh wound. And now I'm crying even harder. How can I possibly explain that watching my beloved church when it split and fell apart last year hurt nearly as much as seeing my parents' marriage crumble?

"I want you to sit right here." Josiah pulls out the chrome kitchen stool with the pink vinyl seat and eases me onto it. And the next thing I know, he's unloading the ice cream cartons from the crate and putting them away in the freezer, which is actually my job. But I feel helpless to stop him as I blot my tears with my handful of organic napkins. Feeling guilty, I glance up at the clock and am relieved to see that I don't have to officially open for business for nearly twenty minutes.

"How did all this happen?" he asks as he rearranges the cartons in the case. "Start at the beginning."

Suddenly I hear myself telling Josiah about how my dad lost his job in real estate when the economy fell apart, how he got really depressed, and how my mom got angry because she had to work harder than ever and it was like my dad was completely paralyzed.

"I know it was really hard on their marriage." I pause to blow my nose. "Even when my dad started to get better, he couldn't find work." I toss the wad of napkins into the trash and take in a deep breath. "Instead he found himself a girlfriend. That was about the same time that our church pretty much fell apart. It started with a disagreement over the budget and turned into this big theological debate that split the church in two." I hold up my hands in a helpless gesture. "So just when we needed it most . . . at least I needed it most—poof—the church was gone."

"That's rough." He nods as he puts the last carton into the case.

"I'm sorry to be such a baby." I reach for a fresh napkin. "I didn't mean to go to pieces on you like that."

Now he places both his hands firmly on my shoulders— again looking directly into my eyes. I feel like my stomach's doing a flip as I look back into his—they are exactly the same color as the espresso gelato. "I asked you to tell me your troubles," he says seriously. "I'm truly glad you did. I care about you, Rachel."

"Really?" My chin trembles, and I'm afraid that I'm going to cry all over again.

"I could tell as soon as I met you that you're a good person, and I've been wanting to know you better."

"Really?" I say again, wishing I could think of a more intelligent response.

He nods. "I'm truly sorry about your parents' divorce, and I know how you feel. My parents split when I was just a kid. It's rough. And I'm sorry about your church letting you down like that." His lips curve into a smile. "But if you'd like to visit a church sometime, you'd be more than welcome to come to ours."

"You have a church?" I don't know why this surprises me, but it does. Maybe it's because the resort workers I've been around so much lately all seem to be a bunch of unchurched, superficial party animals. It's like I forgot there might still be some decent young people around.

"It's my uncle's church. I'm still fairly new to it. I only came to the States a few months ago. But I can assure you it's a good church with good people. And my uncle wants it to grow."

"And it's nearby?" I ask hopefully.

"It's about twenty minutes away."

I frown. "I don't have a car here."

"I can pick you up." He reaches for a napkin and a pen. "Give me your number."

I'm happily telling him my cell phone number when I notice several teenybopper girls standing outside. And now they're banging loudly on the still-locked front door. I glance at the clock to see it's almost eleven now.

"They're a few minutes early, but I should probably let them in before they break the door down."

He pats me on the back. "And I reckon I should finish with my deliveries before the other customers wonder what became of me."

I pull the key ring from my shorts pocket and approach the door, hating to end our conversation and see him go. I reluctantly unlock the glass door, then step away as the girls burst in like they own the place.

"I'll be in touch," he calls from the back of the shop. "You can count on that, Rachel."

I hurry back to the counter and, relieved he's still here, thank him again. "You have no idea how much I needed to have that conversation today," I quietly tell him. "You're truly a godsend."

"You take it easy now." He tips his head politely. "Don't get too hot today. And I'll give you a ring."

For some reason, maybe it's his accent or that he said "ring" instead of "call," but the three girls start giggling even more loudly now. Ignoring their immaturity, I simply wave as Josiah makes his final exit. But when I turn back to the girls, I'm surprised to see they're all staring at me, studying me with what seems like unusual interest.

"Can I help you?" I ask in a no-nonsense tone as I reach for the polka-dot apron, giving it a quick shake before I tie it around my waist. Feeling like I'm about twenty years older than these teeny-boppers, I study their bright-colored outfits and fancy sunglasses. For some reason their "fashionable" attire seems strangely out of place in a rustic lake resort. Honestly, they look more like they dressed to go mall shopping, but you see all kinds around here.

"Your boyfriend looks just like Robert Pattinson," the redhead says to me with wide eyes made dramatic by two garish slashes of electric blue eye shadow.

"Who's Robert Pattinson?" I nonchalantly reach for the vinegar spray and start cleaning the top of the glass case.

Now all three of them laugh hysterically, like I've said the funniest thing ever.

"Are you kidding?" the redhead says. "You don't know who Robert Pattinson is?"

I shrug, then squirt some more spray, wiping the paper towel round and round in fast little circles the way Nadine likes it.

"Robert Pattinson just happens to be the actor who plays Edward in the Twilight series," the skinny blonde girl informs me in a snooty tone.

"Seriously, you'd have to live under a rock not to know *that*," the redhead adds. Again they all laugh, exchanging superior glances among themselves.

Trying to hide the sting of their childish rudeness and remembering how some of my own friends are total Twilight freaks who've made fun of me too, I dramatically sigh and roll my eyes. "Maybe I have better things to do than obsess over a fictional *vampire* character." I hold my head high. "Especially since having a *real live* boyfriend is so much better than merely drooling over a silly actor."

To my relief that comment mostly silences them, and the three girls quickly become distracted with narrowing down their ice cream choices. And yes, I know it's a huge leap to insinuate that Josiah is my boyfriend—and I would be humiliated beyond belief if he'd been close enough to hear my false claim. But I comfort myself that these girls assumed he was my boyfriend first—I simply played along with them. Besides, I decide as I scoop up some pink and blue bubblegum ice cream for the redhead girl, Josiah *could* be my boyfriend . . . someday. Miracles might still happen.

The next hour and a half passes in a blur of tourists of all shapes and sizes with two things in common: (1) they want their ice cream and (2) they want it fast. Even though both fans are running on high and the doors are open, it's already more than ninety degrees in here. It's hot and humid . . . and it smells like a dairy farm. I should've had help by now, but Belinda, as usual, is late.

It's twelve forty-five by the time Belinda arrives at work. And when she waltzes in, the shop is literally hopping. It's like someone in the resort started a rumor that there will be a shortage of ice cream today.

"Sorry I'm a little late," she says glibly as she ties on one of the silly aprons, taking her time to fluff out the bow. Belinda's shift was supposed to start at noon, and although I'm used to her lateness, this seems to be a personal record for her. Unfortunately, I don't feel comfortable complaining since Nadine is her aunt. Instead, I toss a frown her way as I hand a woman a dish of mint chocolate chip ice cream.

"My alarm clock stopped," she says in a slightly whiny tone.

"Can you ring that man up"—I use a damp towel to wipe my sticky hands—"while I dish up the rest of these?" A woman and four little kids are noisily waiting, and I'm eager to get them on their way.

Belinda nods, taking her place by the register, which I know she would rather be running than dipping into the sticky, drippy ice cream.

"Shouldn't Alistair be here by now?" she asks as she hands the man his change. She doesn't bother to count it out the way her aunt has asked us to do. She simply dumps it in his palm, then closes the till with a bang—something else Nadine frowns upon. However, Nadine is not here right now.

"I'm sure he's on his way," I say over my shoulder as I scoop out some butter brickle for one of the little girls. Alistair might not be the sharpest crayon in the box, but at least he's not usually late. And he knows how to count out change. I hand over the butter brickle, then wait as this impatient woman urges the preschool-aged boy to hurry and make up his mind. But when he can't decide, she speaks for him. "Just give him a small scoop of peppermint."

"I don't *want* peppermint!" He stubbornly folds his arms across his front.

"What *do* you want?" I ask him in a friendly tone.

"Benny likes peppermint," the little girl next to him insists.

"Do not!" he yells back at her. "I hate peppermint!"

"Do you like chocolate?" I ask hopefully.

His eyes light up and he nods with enthusiasm.

"No," the woman firmly tells me. "He cannot have chocolate."

Now the boy starts to throw a total fit, claiming he wants chocolate and only chocolate, and I don't know what to do.

"See what you've gone and done?" the woman snarls at me. "Benny *thinks* he likes chocolate, but he really doesn't. If you give it to him, he'll just end up wearing it all over his shirt.

Do you have any idea how hard chocolate stains are to get out?"

I shake my head, forcing a sympathetic smile. "Maybe I should help the next person in line until you guys decide." I glance over her shoulder to where two teen girls are glaring at me with sour expressions.

"No, we were here first," the woman insists. "Just dish up some peppermint and hurry it up."

"Okay." I rinse the scooper and reach into the peppermint carton, which I personally think is disgusting—it reminds me of Pepto-Bismol and I can understand the boy's reluctance. Meanwhile I hear the little boy howling that he doesn't want peppermint. But what am I supposed to do?

"I want *chocolate!*" he screams so loudly my ears begin to ring.

"I think someone needs a nap," the little girl says. I think she's right, but naturally this only makes her brother get louder.

I hurry to shake the scoop of gooey pink into a small dish and quickly hand it to the mother, and then I direct her to the cash register as I ask the girls in line what they want. As they tell me, I resist the urge to scratch my tickly nose. It's one thing to have an itchy nose but something else altogether to wipe sticky ice cream all over your face while amused customers watch. I learned that lesson the hard way.

Of course, by now the little boy (aka brat) is throwing a full-fledged temper tantrum, and after his mom gives Belinda a credit card to pay for the ice cream and tries to placate the kid with the detested peppermint, he responds by hurling the dish of ice cream straight at the window I washed earlier. The dish soundly smacks against the glass and falls to the floor as the lump of ice cream slides down the glass in a long pink stripe of peppermint goop.

"Guess you should've let him have the chocolate," one of the girls says to me as I hand her a double scoop of raspberry gelato.

I shrug. "Tell that to his mother," I say quietly.

"*What* did you say?" the woman demands as she thrusts her signed receipt back toward an amused Belinda. I hadn't realized the mom was still here.

I shrug again. "Nothing . . ."

"I *heard* you." She glares at me. "And I blame you for everything, young lady."

"Me?"

"I think I'll fill out a customer complaint card and report you to the management," she says threateningly. I suddenly grasp why her son is such a brat.

"I didn't do anything wrong." I force myself to remain calm.

"You're the one who brought up the chocolate," she shoots back at me.

"Sorry. It's an option." Turning away from her, I take a deep breath and pick up a fresh scoop, dipping it into the sugar-free vanilla bean. As I hand it to the second girl, I turn back to the grouchy woman. "If it would help, I can give your son a free dish of chocolate ice cream."

"Yeah!" the boy yells. "I want the chocolate."

She rolls her eyes, telling her kids to get outside as she attempts to herd them toward the door. But the little boy isn't budging. Instead he presses his grimy hands and face against the glass front of the case, insisting he wants the chocolate. So I quickly dip a small scoop, and despite the fact that his mother is ignoring me now, I hand the dish to him.

"Enjoy!" I tell him with a fixed smile. And to my relief, he leaves.

"Nice work," Belinda says in a sarcastic tone, "now let's just hope he doesn't have allergies and his mom decides to sue us."

The teen girls laugh, and I try not to look worried. But after seeing that mother deal with her kids, it wouldn't surprise me if she ran out to find a lawyer or complained to the management of the resort. On one hand, I'm not sure I'd mind losing this job. But my mom would be disappointed. And there goes my college fund.

Also there's Josiah to consider. If I go back home, how will I ever get to know him better? How will I get to visit his church? And meet his uncle? Thinking of Josiah makes it easier for me to smile and act congenial toward the customers. And ironically, it seems that they begin to smile and act more congenially to me.

Alistair arrives right at one, and soon the three of us are working like crazy as the pace settles into a frenetic rush. As the temperature rises, so does everyone's craving for natural ice cream. The upside of being this busy is the time goes by quickly. And to my relief, it's soon three o'clock, and Nadine shows up to work on the books and oversee things—it's also time for my "lunch" break and not a moment too soon.

As I go outside, where the triple-digit temps have hit, I remember what Josiah said about jumping in the lake. I look down at my now-grimy uniform and the usual droplets of ice cream spotted on my legs and tennis shoes. And without considering what it must look like, I walk down to the dock, going clear out to the end, and simply jump off. The cold water takes my breath away and I come up sputtering. There, sitting in a sailboat and wearing swimsuits, are some of the girls who bought ice cream earlier. Naturally, they are laughing at me.

"Rough day at the ice cream parlor?" one of them calls.

I just nod and, turning away, proceed to swim toward shore, which is awkward in tennis shoes. But eventually I make it, walking out with water pouring from my clothes. And that's when I remember—I forgot to take my iPhone out of my pocket. I check to see if it's still there. It is. But as I shake the water out of it and attempt to turn it on, I can see that it no longer works.

CHAPTER 3

s I walk over to the Greek kiosk to order my usual gyro for lunch, I realize that no cell phone means that Josiah cannot call me now. While I eat my gyro, I come up with what might actually be a good backup plan. I will call him instead.

By the time I return to work, my uniform is almost completely dry, and really, I don't think anyone could even guess that I jumped into the lake an hour ago. Maybe I'll start doing that every day.

"Your mom called during your lunch break," Nadine tells me as I tie on my little apron. "She said she tried your cell phone."

I sigh. "It got wet. It's not working now."

"Well, she's decided to come up here for the weekend."

"My mom's coming up here?" I'm not sure if I like this idea.

"It's the Fourth on Sunday, so Monday is a holiday . . . well, not for us, of course." Nadine pauses to write something down on her ever-present notepad. "And the fireworks on the lake are spectacular. I told Bev she should come and see it. She's going to stay with me in the condo." Nadine frowns at me. "You okay with that?"

I shrug. "Of course. Mom can do what she wants."

"I know you usually have Sundays and Mondays off, but I hoped you'd be willing to work — "

"But I already made plans," I tell her.

"Plans?" Her brow creases again.

"I'm going to church on Sunday."

She waves her hand. "Oh, well, that's okay. You can work *after* church. And since it's a holiday, I'll pay you time and a half for both Sunday and Monday." She points to her office. "Now you better call your mom and let her know your phone's not working so she doesn't get worried."

I start to point out that I talked to her this morning, but why bother? Instead I call Mom and, without going into detail, explain that my phone got wet, and she promises to bring me a spare phone when she comes up for the weekend. "Maybe you can stay at Nadine's too," she suggests.

"I don't think so." There's no way I'm going to spend a night at Nadine's. "It'll already be crowded with you and Belinda staying with her. I'm fine at the dorm." Never mind that she has four long-haired cats in her "cozy" two-bedroom condo. Then I tell Mom that I'm going to church that morning.

"That's nice," she says in a tone that suggests she has absolutely no interest in hearing more about this. Which is perfectly fine with me because I don't want to tell her about Josiah anyway. No need to stir up any unnecessary curiosity with her.

I can just imagine her demanding to know everything — like who is he, how old is he, what are his intentions? But thinking of Josiah reminds me that I need to get the dairy's phone number. So while Mom rattles on about someone in her office, I flip through Nadine's Rolodex. Finding the number for the Lost Springs Dairy, I jot it down for later use and slip it in my pocket, right next to my useless phone.

The rest of my shift continues to be as busy — and as hot — as it was earlier. As usual, Nadine leaves just as Lorna arrives for work at six. Lorna only works evenings, although Belinda is plotting to have Lorna trade shifts with me since she and Lorna seem to have become fast friends and Lorna makes no secret about wanting to get more hours.

My shift ends at six thirty, nine hours after I arrived this morning, and as I'm getting ready to toss my apron into the laundry hamper, I decide to say something to Lorna. Belinda is on her lunch break, and this might be my best chance to get Lorna's attention. "I don't mean to complain," I tell her as I fill in my time card, barely looking at her, "but when I got here this morning, the soft yogurt machine was really a mess."

Lorna lets out an exasperated sigh. "I cleaned it out as usual last night."

"Maybe as usual isn't good enough."

She narrows her eyes. "It was perfectly clean, Rachel. I don't see why you need to make such a big deal about everything." She looks over at Alistair now. "I cleaned it like usual, *didn't I*, Alistair?"

He nods nervously. I can tell by his eyes that he might have a different opinion, but I also know that Lorna's strong personality overwhelms him.

"I'm not trying to turn this into a big deal," I tell Lorna. "I'm just saying that the machines need to be cleaned better. Unless you want some of Nadine's customers to get sick."

She laughs. "No one's going to get sick."

"Maybe Alistair should clean out the machines."

"Fine," she snaps at me. "Alistair, you're in charge of cleaning the machines from now on."

Alistair blinks, then nods. But as I'm leaving, I sense him giving me a scowl, like it's my fault he's been saddled with this new responsibility. Why do kids get jobs if they don't want to work? Seriously, what is wrong with people? But instead of obsessing over these annoyances, I set out to find a pay phone . . . if such a thing even exists here. Finally I ask one of the security guards, and he points me over to a kiosk where there is an ATM, a U.S. mailbox, and an old-fashioned pay phone.

Feeling nervous, I dial the number, and when a woman politely says, "Hello, this is Lost Springs Dairy, can I help you?" I get tongue-tied. For some reason I expected Josiah to answer.

"I, uh . . . I . . ."

"Can I help you?" she says again.

"I'm sorry. I was trying to reach Josiah."

"Josiah's not here," she says crisply.

"Yes, well, I gave Josiah my cell phone number. He told me about his church and I wanted to visit, but now my cell phone is broken and I'm actually using a pay phone and I . . . uh . . ." I don't know what more to say.

"You're interested in our church?" she asks with a bit more warmth.

"Yes, I work at Rock Canyon Lake, and I've really missed going to church. I wanted to go on Sunday. But I'm worried he'll try to call my cell phone and it won't work. I will have a new one . . . eventually."

So now she takes my name, and I suggest that Josiah might be able to call me at Nadine's shop. I even tell her my hours. "Except on Sunday. I told my boss that I planned to go to church," I say quickly. "She said that's okay."

"All right then. I'll be sure to let Josiah know."

"Thank you!" I say eagerly. "I appreciate it."

"And my name is Celeste Davis. I'm Josiah's aunt."

"Oh, so it's your husband who's the pastor?"

"That's right. I hope to meet you on Sunday, Rachel."

I thank her again, and feeling satisfied I say good-bye and hang up. Really, what more can I do? If the pastor's wife, Josiah's aunt, knows I want to visit their church, it seems like a done deal. Or so I hope.

· · · · · · · · · ·

Friday at Nadine's is as hot and miserable and busy as the previous day. Maybe even worse. And despite my second plunge into the cold lake during my lunch break earlier, I feel like a nasty, smelly dishrag as I finish my shift at six thirty. It doesn't improve matters to know that no one is sad to see me go as I drop my time card into the slot. Seriously, it's starting to feel like my coworkers have all turned against me. And simply because I like doing a good job — and they don't seem to care.

If Belinda wasn't Nadine's niece, I think I would report all of them as lazy and worthless. Oh, Alistair would probably be an okay employee, except that he's so easily influenced by Lorna and Belinda. But even if I did tell, it would probably just wind up being my word against Belinda's in the end. And although my mom and Nadine are friends, I'm sure Nadine's allegiance would rest with her own flesh and blood. So why bother?

As I trudge back toward the dorm, which should be pretty quiet on a Friday night, I wonder why I even care about keeping Nadine's clean and sanitary in the first place. Why not just turn into a slacker like the rest of her employees? Who cares?

"Rachel!"

I turn to see a guy jogging down the boardwalk toward me. I am pleasantly surprised when I realize it's Josiah! And instead of wearing his usual dairyman delivery uniform, tonight he's got on a madras plaid shirt, khaki shorts, and sandals.

"Hey." I wave happily, hurrying to meet him. "What are you doing here?"

"I came to see you."

Now I'm painfully aware of my messy appearance, not to mention I probably smell like a cow. But he works at a dairy, so maybe he won't notice. "I, uh, just finished my shift at the ice cream shop."

"I know." He nods. "My aunt told me you called and that your phone's on the blink."

I hold out my hands as an explanation for my shoddy appearance. "I was just heading back to the dorm to clean up."

"Awesome. I'd love to see you in civilian clothes."

"Really?"

He laughs. "Absolutely. How about you get yourself cleaned up and then we'll go grab a bite to eat?"

I nod, trying not to look as surprised as I feel. "It won't take me long," I assure him. "I can get myself together in about twenty minutes."

"Beaut." But now he gives me a doubtful look. "That's pretty fast for a sheila. Are you certain?"

"Yes. Half an hour tops—and that's only if the showers are busy, which shouldn't be the case."

"You do that and you might just be my dream girl."

My heart does a flip-flop now, and to my relief, we're in front of the big dorm building. "This is it. There's a community room if you want to wait in—"

"No worries." He points to the bench in front. "I'll just wait here."

Then I rush into the dorm, and as I'm running down the

hall to the women's section, I begin to unbutton my shirt.

"Someone's in a hurry," a girl teases me as I dash past her. "Hot date?"

Ignoring her, I grab my shower stuff and continue stripping off my clothes as I head for the bathroom. Thankfully, there's an unoccupied shower and I make record time getting clean. Drying myself as I rush back to get dressed, I realize I don't have the luxury of obsessing over what I'm going to wear or changing my outfit several times. Instead I pull out my blue-and-white checked sundress. It almost always makes me feel happy when I wear it. Then I shove my feet into my favorite Gap sandals, and letting my still-damp hair fall loosely around my shoulders, I fluff it with my fingers.

I grab my purse and paw through it as I walk back down the hall. I pause in front of the big mirror next to the front door to apply some lip gloss and mascara and give my hair one last fluff. Not bad for such short notice.

"How was that?" I ask Josiah, trying not to show how relieved I am that he's still here . . . that I didn't imagine the whole scenario.

He holds up his phone to show the time. "Incredible. That was exactly nineteen minutes and forty seconds, Rachel." Now he peers more closely at me. "And you look fantastic!" He reaches for my hand. "You truly are my dream girl."

I laugh as we walk together.

"I called some of the resort restaurants." He leads us back toward the main part of town. "Sounds like almost everyone is booked for hours. But I did find one that's willing to take us. If we hurry."

"Considering this is a holiday weekend and a Friday, that's quite an accomplishment. Well, unless it's one of the kiosks."

I smile at him. "And even if we eat at Frank's Frankfurters, I won't complain." The truth is, I would happily sit on the side of the lake and eat a can of tuna fish with this guy.

"Are you for real?" he asks.

"I was just wondering the same thing about you." I laugh. "I mean, you show up out of the blue and what was going to be a boring night suddenly gets interesting." It gets even more interesting when he leads me up to Frederico's Italian restaurant.

"Here we go."

"Are you sure?" I ask as he opens the big wooden door. "This place is usually hard to get into."

"They had a cancellation. The woman said if we got here within five minutes, it was ours."

"Awesome." As he goes up to the hostess, I'm glad I brought my purse. This restaurant is expensive and I'm not assuming he's going to pay for both of us. And I don't even care if we go dutch — or if I end up paying for both of us. I think I'd give up a whole week's pay for this evening. Well, maybe not a whole week. But at least a few days.

The restaurant is crowded, and the hostess leads us past several filled tables. It all looks very elegant with white linens, fresh flowers, glistening silver, sparkling glassware, flickering candles. I take it all in, trying to memorize each detail so I can play it back later. She finally settles us at a quiet corner table that's not even next to the kitchen.

"Here you go." She waits for us to sit, then politely hands us oversized menus and fills our water glasses. "Your waitress will be with you shortly."

I smile at Josiah. "This place is perfection."

"I hope the food is as good as everything else."

"I can hardly believe that less than an hour ago, I was up to my elbows in drippy ice cream," I confess.

"Don't you love it when life takes you around an unexpected corner?"

I nod happily. "I do."

I nearly fall out of my chair when Steffie, the short blonde from my dorm, steps up to take our order. "I thought you worked at the Blue Moose Café," I say dumbly. She looks nearly as stunned to see me as I am to see her. "I have *two* jobs," she informs me with a stiff little smile.

"Oh . . . I didn't know." I feel a little guilty for not being more friendly.

After placing our orders — I'm careful to order one of the cheapest meals: linguini with pesto, which is actually one of my favorites — I decide this is my opportunity to find out more about Josiah. As soon as Steffie departs, I start peppering him with questions. I quickly learn that he's been in "the States," as he calls our country, for five months.

"My mum thinks I'm on a mission."

"A mission?" I'm confused now.

"It's for the GEF church."

It takes me a moment to remember what GEF stands for. But then it hits me — like a sucker punch. I should've known. This felt too good to be true, and now it's falling apart right before my eyes. "You mean you're part of the God's Eternal Family church?" I ask meekly.

"No, no, not me. Not anymore, that is. But my mum is pretty devout."

A wave of relief rushes over me. I'm not sure what I would've done if Josiah had turned out to be a member of a cult church. Not that I have anything against those people personally. I even knew a girl who went to a GEF church. She seemed really nice, until I realized she was only trying to get me to come to her church. But I already knew about GEF. My church had warned against getting involved with GEF . . . back before it fell to pieces.

"That's what broke up my parents' marriage," he explains. "My dad was fed up with her church. After he left, my mum remarried a bloke who's a rock-solid GEF. He's a deacon."

"Did you live with them? I mean, your mom and stepdad?"

"I did for a while. Then I started to question some of their beliefs and the church." He shakes his head. "That didn't go over too well with my stepdad. He said I was a bad influence on my sisters."

"Sisters?"

"Yeah, I have three younger sisters. How about you? Any siblings?"

I shake my head no. "I always felt cheated by that. I used to wish I was part of a big family. How old are your sisters?"

His brow creases. "Let's see, I reckon Vera is sixteen, Corrine is fourteen, and Beth is eleven."

"Do you miss them?"

He shrugs. "Yeah, I guess so . . . sometimes. Except that they're all brainwashed and into the church, just like my mum and stepdad. Nice little GEF girls. My stepdad was absolutely certain I was going to corrupt them. That's why I went to live with my dad in Sydney. My dad's no saint, but there was a lot less yelling there. More peace and quiet."

I nod. "I can understand that."

"When my mum heard I was coming to the States, she got all worked up. Probably because I'm her only son. She was certain she was losing me for good, and she literally made herself sick with worry." He gives me a lopsided grin. "That's why I told her I was going on a mission . . . you know, to ease her mind."

"What kind of mission does she think you're on?"

"Oh, just the usual — traveling around with another bloke, telling people about the GEF church. It's what the church expects blokes to do after they finish secondary school. Two years on the mission field. It's supposed to solidify their faith." He's playing with his butter knife like it's a drumstick, and judging by his expression I suspect he feels guilty for deceiving his mother.

"Will you ever tell her the truth?"

"Oh, sure . . . someday. But if she knew what I was really doing . . ." He sadly shakes his head. "Well, she'd be pretty upset."

"Just because you're working at a dairy instead of converting people to God's Eternal Family?"

He chuckles. "That too, but she'd be truly miffed to find out I'm working at my uncle's dairy. My mum cannot stand Uncle Jim."

"That's the uncle who owns the dairy?"

He nods. "Jim is my dad's brother. He left the GEF church ages ago. My mum calls Jim the 'filthy black sheep.' And she claims he's the reason my dad left the church. If she knew I was here with Uncle Jim" — he stops drumming with the silverware — "it would not be good."

"But didn't you say that your uncle started a church? He must be a good man to start his own church. You'd think your mother would appreciate that."

"But it's not a GEF church," he explains. "She'd rather I didn't belong to any church. She'd rather I went out drinking every night."

"I don't get it. I mean, on one hand it reminds me of some of the stubbornness I saw when my church split. People who were like 'it's my way or the highway.'" I shake my head. "But seriously, why are people like that?"

"Good question."

"So, you're done with school . . ." I study him. "How old are you?"

"I'll be twenty in August."

I try not to look surprised, but twenty sounds old.

"How about you?"

Suddenly I'm worried. If I tell him I'm only seventeen, he might drop me like a bad habit. And then I'll never get to really know him. In the same instant, I remember something my grandmother always writes in my birthday cards, telling me that I've entered a new year—when I turned seventeen last fall she wrote, "You're in your eighteenth year."

"I'm eighteen," I proclaim as if it's true. "My eighteenth year . . . which according to my grandmother means I'm supposed to start acting like an adult." I laugh nervously. "Sometimes that's not so easy."

"You can say that again."

Relieved to have that lie behind me, I try to suppress the guilt by changing the subject. "How long has your uncle been running the dairy?"

"I'm not sure. He came to the States when I was still a kid. I reckon it was about twelve or thirteen years ago that he bought the ranch. It had been a dairy, but I guess it was pretty run-down. It's taken a lot of work to get it into shape. But it's real nice now. Uncle Jim has done some amazing upgrades. And his goal is to be completely self-sufficient and off the grid."

"No electricity?"

"Right. He's already experimenting with solar and geothermal and wind power. But the dairy has a lot of machinery to run."

"It sounds interesting."

"It is. And it's really a great piece of property. About four hundred acres total. It's tucked into the mountains, but with lots of green meadows as well as timber. And Lost Springs Creek runs right through the middle of it."

"It sounds beautiful. I'd love to see it."

He nods. "You will see it if you still want to come to church on Sunday."

"I can't wait."

He looks directly into my eyes. "It's refreshing to meet a girl who is excited about something like going to church." He chuckles. "I mean, a girl who's not with God's Eternal Family."

I shake my head. "I'm definitely not into GEF." Now I shrug. "I don't even know what I am really. I just believe in God and Jesus and the Bible."

"So do we," he tells me. "Don't you think that's enough?"

Now Steffie brings us our salads and a basket of bread, and to my delight, Josiah bows his head and asks a sincere humble blessing before we eat. Honestly, I almost feel like I've died and gone to heaven. Is this guy for real?

As we eat dinner, which turns out to be delicious, I confess to Josiah that I'm a foodie.

"What's a foodie?" he asks.

"Someone who thoroughly enjoys food."

He frowns. "But you're not fat."

I laugh. "Well, thank you. But it's not like that. I enjoy learning about food and cooking."

His eyes light up. "You really are my dream girl."

Every time he says this, I feel so happy I could burst into song. But instead of making a fool of myself, I tell him about my secret dream. "I want to own and run a restaurant." I glance around the elegant dining room. "Not exactly like Frederico's, although this is really nice. I want a traditional sort of restaurant. And very uptown. I'm not really sure what it will be like. Except that it will be big and gorgeous and successful."

"That's quite a dream."

"My mom thinks it's crazy. She's a bookkeeper and some of her clients own restaurants. She's always telling me how miserable they are. She says they never get time off and they're always about to go under." I spread some butter on a piece of warm crusty bread. "In fact, I'm sure that's why she talked me into coming to work for Nadine. She thought it would be such a bad experience that I'd give up my dream altogether."

"But Nadine's isn't exactly a restaurant."

I nod, chewing. "I know. And I've worked in restaurants before. But because Nadine's is small, I'm getting the chance to do some management things." I roll my eyes. "At least that was how it was supposed to be. Most of the time it feels more like babysitting." Now I tell him about the lazy employees. "Nadine's niece is the worst. But how can I complain about her?"

"That's got to be rough."

"I just hope it doesn't all blow up in my face before summer's over." I glance around the dining room again. "But maybe I could get a job in a place like this. Although I've heard that's not easy to do. According to Nadine, a lot of the businesses over-hire at the beginning of summer and start letting the slackers go after the Fourth."

"Maybe Nadine will let some of her slackers go too."

"I doubt that."

"What else do you like to do?" he asks. "Any hobbies?"

"I'll tell you if you promise not to make fun of me."

His dark brows arch with interest. "Why would I make fun of you?"

"Because a lot my so-called friends tease me."

"I would never do that."

"Do you know what 4-H is?"

He shakes his head as he forks into his four-cheese raviolis.

So, trying not to feel like a nerd, I explain. "The four Hs stand for head, heart, hands, and health."

"That sounds interesting, but what does it mean?"

"The 4-H pledge might explain it better." Feeling even more like a nerd, I repeat the old pledge for him: "I pledge my head to clearer thinking. My heart to greater loyalty. My hands to larger service. And my health to better living, for my club, my community, my country, and my world."

"I like that." He tilts his head to one side. "Why did you think I'd tease you about it?"

I shrug. "Some people think it's geeky." I tell him about some of the projects I've been involved with over the years.

"4-H sounds like a great organization. In some ways it reminds me of what my uncle is trying to do with his church."

"Really?"

He nods eagerly. "The jobs at the dairy provide work for members of his congregation. And he's fully committed to healthy living by producing natural organic dairy products. When you meet him, you should tell him about your 4-H pledge. I'm sure he'd be interested to hear about it."

I resist the urge to pinch myself, but I can hardly believe that a guy this cool is excited about something like 4-H. Maybe the world is changing.

After dinner, we take the trail that goes around the lake, walking and talking for more than an hour. But by nine thirty, we're back in front of the dorm and Josiah tells me he has to get home. "My uncle let me use his car tonight, but his curfew is ten."

"And I have to work in the morning," I tell him.

"So do I."

I stand there looking at him, and his face looks even more handsome illuminated by the lamplight. "Thanks so much for a perfect evening."

"Thank *you*, Rachel." He reaches out to tenderly touch my cheek, and electric tingles run up and down my spine. I do not want this moment to end.

"It's great getting to know you better," I say quietly.

And then he leans down and kisses me gently but firmly on the lips. But just like that, the kiss ends. He grins, and then, tipping his head, he waves and takes off, jogging down the boardwalk. All I can do is stand there, with weak knees, watching as he disappears into the shadows. Is any of this real . . . or just a lovely, lovely dream?

. . . .

On Saturday, I feel like I'm walking on clouds and I refuse to let anything or anyone bring me down. Naturally since it's a holiday weekend, we are busier than ever. And Lorna has been scheduled for a full day, which could prove aggravating, except that I won't let it. Even when we're super busy and the shop is hotter than ever, I smile and treat every customer like royalty, and to my pleased surprise, they seem to respond with a bit more manners and patience. Or maybe it's just me.

When Nadine comes in at three, I'm caught off guard to see my mom with her. Then I remember that she came up for the weekend. We exchange hugs and I introduce her to the crew, acting as if we're all chummy friends.

"I thought you and your mom might like to take your lunch break together," Nadine tells me.

"And Nadine said you can have more than an hour if you want," Mom says. "Enough time to show me around the resort."

"Are you sure?" I ask Nadine.

She waves me off. "No problem. Take your time."

"Thanks." As I remove the apron, I sense Lorna watching me with what looks like envy, or maybe it's just curiosity. The fact that Mom is a blue-eyed blonde and I am part African-American sometimes catches friends by surprise. Not that I'd classify Lorna as a friend. Anyway, I smile and give a little finger wave, grab my purse, and make a quick exit.

"I got settled in at Nadine's," Mom says as we go outside, "but I haven't really had a chance to look around."

"And it was dark when you dropped me off here in June." I lead us down to the lake and marina.

"I didn't realize it was so pretty." She puts on her sunglasses and smiles. "What a lovely place to spend a summer."

I'm tempted to complain, but I don't want to go down that trail. Instead, as I show her around, I sing the praises of Rock Canyon Lake Resort like I'm part of the official welcoming committee or selling real estate.

We snag an outdoor table at the Blue Moose Café for lunch, but when I see Steffie working here, I get worried. What if she waits on our table, and what if she says something about last night . . . or mentions the great-looking guy I was with? For some reason I am not ready to tell my mom about Josiah yet.

As we peruse the menu, I ask myself why I don't want her to know. But it doesn't take long to figure it out. She'll ask questions and eventually want to know his age. If I say he's nearly twenty, she'll freak. I know she will. For now, I want to keep Josiah all to myself. It will be simpler that way.

Fortunately, Steffie isn't working this area, so my secret is safe. In time, I will tell Mom all about him. Maybe after my eighteenth birthday . . . or after Josiah proposes to me. I smile as I set the menu aside. Okay, neither Josiah nor I are ready for marriage, but it's still fun to think about. And someday, maybe after a year or two of college, or after I've just opened my new restaurant — someday I'll be ready for that.

"You seem happy, Rachel." Mom sips her iced tea, studying me.

"I am happy."

"I'm glad to see that. I was a little worried about you the other morning."

"You mean when you told me the news about you and Dad?" I frown. "You didn't really expect me to be happy about *that,* did you?"

"No, I realize that you wish we were still together." She stirs her drink with her straw.

"Don't you wish you were too?"

She shrugs. "I don't know. Maybe it's for the best."

"Are you *serious?*" Okay, I tell myself—do not go there right now. Do not start an argument with your mom. Remember how happy you are . . . stay in this happy place. I remember how Josiah told his mom he was on a mission, just to keep her from worrying. Surely, I can keep my mouth shut about this.

"I know you don't agree with me, Rachel. You think that marriages are supposed to last forever."

"Aren't they?" I keep my tone soft, not like I'm trying to start a debate, more like I'm just curious. "I mean, didn't you think it was going to be forever when you and Dad got married?"

"Of course. And he did too. But people change."

I nod. "I know."

"And I suppose you're right, Rachel."

"About what?"

"If I could have my wish, I do wish your dad and I could get back together."

"Really?"

She nods in a sad way. "But it's not going to happen. You know he's been dating Selena."

"I know." Selena is the part of this equation I try not to think about. Never mind that she's fifteen years younger than my dad or that she's drop-dead gorgeous (in that Barbie sort of way). But I honestly think the most aggravating part about Selena is that she has money. Well, that and my dad. Sometimes I wonder, if Selena didn't have her huge alimony settlement and a big house and a great job, maybe my dad wouldn't have been so attracted to her. Or maybe I'm just naive.

"Well, I heard from Linda Allen that your father has moved in with Selena."

I blink and set down my soda. "Seriously?"

She just nods. "Sounds like he moved in with her even before the divorce was final. Linda said his excuse was that Selena needed someone to stay with her boys."

"So Dad is living at her house? Taking care of those monsters?" I can't believe I used to babysit for Selena, that I used to consider her to be my friend.

"Can you imagine it? Your father chasing around after those two boys? What are their names again? I know they always sounded like cowboy names."

"Tex and Wade. Tex must be five by now. And Wade must be close to four." I remember chasing after them in Selena's big house. "I'll bet they can run even faster now."

Mom almost smiles. "Well, there's some satisfaction knowing your father will have his hands full with those two. Can you imagine him playing Mr. Mom?"

I shake my head. "My imagination isn't that clever." Now despite my resolve to continue enjoying my high from last night, I feel depressed. The news that Dad has moved in with Selena is truly disturbing. Still, I don't want to make Mom feel any worse. So I make a few lame jokes about how exhausted my dad must be by the end of the day. "What if Selena expects him to do the laundry, clean, and fix meals?"

"Your father's housekeeping skills are nonexistent. The helpless man barely knows how to boil water."

"I know."

"So you can see, I'm not feeling much hope that our marriage will ever be restored," she says after our food arrives. "Mostly I want to get on with my life, Rachel. I'm sorry you get stuck with divorced parents and all that. But we both just need to move on now."

I nod as I bite into my portabella-mushroom sandwich.

"I realize that your father is still your father," she says as she forks into her Cobb salad, "no matter what kind of stupid choices he makes. And I don't ever want to make you choose between us, Rachel."

"Don't worry. I know that. The truth is, I really don't want to have anything to do with Dad right now. I mean, I know I'll have to forgive him . . . eventually. But right now, well, I'd rather not think about him." I take a sip of soda. "And I doubt I'm even on his radar these days."

"Don't be so sure. I'll bet he'd *love* to have you visit. You could give him a hand with those wild little boys or even teach him to cook."

Now that actually makes me laugh. "Fat chance. In fact, if he ever does invite me to come see him, I'll have to think about it long and hard before I commit."

Mom seems in good spirits as we walk back to Nadine's. I can tell she's relieved that I'm not obsessing over the divorce. Admittedly, that has as much to do with thinking about Josiah as anything else. Not that I'm planning to divulge that to her.

"I almost forgot," she says when we reach Nadine's. She digs in her bag, then pulls out her old flip phone. "I got this activated for you. It's not the greatest and it always seems to need recharging, but it's better than nothing."

I nod and slip the phone into my purse as Mom goes inside. "Thanks." At least Josiah will be able to reach me now. That's something.

"My goodness, it's warm in here," Mom says as I'm tying on my apron.

"The AC is broken," Nadine tells her. "I've got a man coming in next week. But in the meantime . . ." She sighs as she fans herself with a paper plate, blotting perspiration from her forehead with a napkin. She turns to me. "I know I usually stay until six, but since your mom is here, I'm giving myself the rest of the afternoon off. You're in charge, Rachel."

And just like that, they're gone.

Lorna and Belinda both start acting like they're getting paid to stand around and complain about the unbearable heat. Meanwhile, Alistair and I are scooping like mad. Although Belinda is running the cash register, Lorna is definitely slacking.

"Maybe you should just take your lunch break," I tell her. "Since you're not doing anything anyway."

"I was just about to make some more waffle dishes." She glares at me. "Since someone forgot to make any fresh ones this morning."

"I made three dozen," I protest. "And then it got too busy to make more."

"Three dozen?" She looks skeptical. "Yeah, right."

"Here." I slap the scoop into her hand. "Why don't you take over for me here, and I'll make some more right now."

"I don't want to scoop," she argues.

"Did you hear Nadine?" I lock gazes with her. "I'm in charge. And you're on scoop duty now."

She grumbles but complies. And I wonder why she doesn't appreciate the switch. It might be sticky business scooping ice cream, but it's a whole lot cooler than making waffle dishes. But why did I think she'd appreciate it?

I'm just finishing my tenth waffle dish when the business line rings, and since I'm in charge, I answer it. Naturally, I can't hide my pleasure when I hear Josiah's voice on the other end. And, of course, my cheerful greeting gets everyone's attention. I can tell they're all listening.

"I just wanted to be sure you still want to come to church tomorrow," he says.

"Absolutely." I use my free hand to fill the hot waffle-dish maker with more batter. "Can't wait."

"If you don't mind, I'll pick you up at eight thirty. Service doesn't start until ten, but that'll give me time to show you around some."

"Great!"

"Well, I know you're working so I won't keep you."

"Thanks. I'll see you tomorrow—" I stop myself from saying his name. I so don't want these guys to guess who it is I'm seeing. No, for now, Josiah is my secret. Mine alone. And the longer I can keep it that way, the happier I will be.

Nadine's is still überbusy when my shift ends at six thirty. But it's nothing that three people can't handle if they do it right. Even so, Belinda makes a fuss as I toss my apron into the hamper.

"You're going to leave us when we're swamped like this?"

"My shift is over." I drop my time card into its slot. "My mom is picking me up for dinner at Nadine's. And I still need to get back to the dorm to clean up first."

"La-tee-dah," Lorna taunts. "Aren't we so very special?"

Ignoring her nastiness, as well as Belinda's narrowed eyes, I grab my purse and make a hasty exit. I might've been in charge during my shift, but it's up to Belinda to hold it together now. I hate to even imagine what kind of condition this place will be in by Sunday. To say I was unimpressed with the sanitation when I opened this morning would be an understatement. Fortunately, I won't be opening the shop tomorrow. I will be in church.

As I walk to my dorm, I decide it's time to blow the whistle on Nadine's lazy crew. She has a right to know. And perhaps it will be easier to bring it up with my mom nearby to buffer things. After all, what if Nadine's customers got some form of food poisoning due to poorly cleaned equipment? What if someone sued her? Or what if the health department shut her business down and fined her?

Yes, it's high time Nadine finds out what kind of people she has working for her. And it's up to me to tell her. If she doesn't believe me, she can check her security surveillance video. Not that I expect she'll do that. But that camera is working the whole time we're there. Surely it would reveal what sort of job they're doing — rather what they're not doing — before closing.

I t's not until after dinner that I broach the subject of Nadine's useless employees. I actually used my mom as a sounding board when she picked me up, and now I'm taking her advice to "go carefully."

"I don't want to bash anyone," I tell Nadine, "but I'm worried that without proper sanitation of the machines and food preparation surfaces, we'll be at risk of a food-borne illness outbreak and you could be out of business."

Nadine looks surprised. "I can see that someone took her food handler's training seriously."

"Rachel has always been interested in these things," Mom tells her. "She's been studying up in 4-H for years now."

"We used to have a food booth at the county fair," I explain. "We had to be careful." Then I tell her how the health inspector came by regularly to make sure everything was sanitary and safe. "But honestly, if an inspector had come into the ice cream shop this morning, we would've been in trouble."

"Perhaps the girls who close don't know how to properly clean," Mom suggests. "Maybe they need a refresher course."

"Yes, that's a good idea." Nadine looks at me. "Maybe you should be the one to teach it."

I try not to grimace. "Maybe . . . except I'm not sure they'll listen to me."

"Why not?"

I shrug, glancing nervously at Mom.

"Perhaps it would help if you both gave them a refresher course," Mom says. "They might respect it more coming from you, Nadine."

Nadine seems to buy this. "I have a plan. Why don't we all go over there right before closing time? Rachel can teach them how to properly clean the machines and close shop." She nods to Mom. "And you and I will supervise."

As unenthused as I feel about Nadine's plan, I agree. At 9:55, we show up at the shop, which still has a couple of customers. After the customers leave, Nadine locks the doors and announces the plan.

"I realize it's quitting time," she tells them. "But Rachel has informed me that we could be in violation of the health department's requirements."

"What?" Belinda looks shocked.

"Apparently the cleaning has been substandard," Nadine tells her. "Now I'm not pointing the finger at anyone, but I decided it's time for a refresher course on how to clean and close." She points to me now. "Go ahead, Rachel."

"Rachel is going to teach us?" Lorna frowns.

"Rachel was in 4-H," Nadine tells them. Naturally, both Belinda and Lorna laugh. Even Alistair snickers. "Rachel knows all about these things and is happy to share her insight with us."

"I'll bet she is," Belinda says quietly.

"Go ahead, Rachel." Nadine pulls out a stool and an office chair for herself and my mom.

I can tell by my fellow employees' expressions that they all want to kill me. I'm sure they had hoped to get out of here fast. After all, it's a Saturday night. And living at the dorm, I'm well aware there are all kinds of things going on tonight—stupid drinking parties and whatnot—that these three were probably looking forward to participating in.

"This doesn't have to take long," I begin. And giving them various cleanup tasks, I attempt to remedy what's been neglected of late. I remind them of the importance of using the bleach-water solution to kill bacteria. "Dairy products are prone to food-borne illnesses like salmonella, shigella, or E. coli. But a good wash-down with a bleach solution will kill those bacteria."

Lorna rolls her eyes, but I ignore her as I continue. "See this cutting board?" I hold up a large cutting board where we chop fruit for smoothies and toppings. "It needs to be cleaned with the bleach solution throughout the day. Just like all the surfaces."

It takes nearly forty minutes to do a thorough cleaning, and I can tell that everyone, including my mom, has had more than enough of my refresher course. But really, is it my fault no one's been doing it correctly? "I don't think it should take that long tomorrow night," I tell them as we're leaving. "It's just that I want you all to really understand how to do this right . . . and how important it is."

However, I can tell by their stony silence and the dagger looks—even Alistair is sulky—they couldn't care less. And worse than that, I suspect they'll make me pay for this . . . later.

"I'll just walk back to my dorm," I tell Mom and Nadine as we're locking up. "And don't forget I'm going to church tomorrow. I won't be in to work until the afternoon."

Nadine just nods. And Mom gives me a tired wave. As I walk to the dorm, I feel totally underappreciated. My one consolation is that Josiah is coming in the morning. I will have several blissful hours with him before I have to face the music with my fellow workers at Nadine's.

· · · · · · · · · ·

Josiah is right on time the following morning. And I am ready and waiting, standing outside the dorm wearing a floral-print skirt and a yellow shirt.

"You look as fresh as a daisy," Josiah tells me as I climb into the small hybrid car.

"Thank you." I grin, taking in his pale blue shirt and navy pants. "You look very handsome yourself."

"Fortunately, my uncle doesn't make us wear ties. Not like my mum's stuffy old church. But he does insist on long pants and button-up shirts for men. And, of course, dresses for women."

"Oh, I hope this is okay." I look down at my skirt, relieved that I didn't wear pants, which I nearly did.

"No worries there. You're a guest today. You get to wear whatever you like."

As he drives, I spill out the story of my previous evening and how I made my coworkers angry last night. "I'm almost afraid to go to work today."

"You'd think they'd appreciate that you took the time to help them."

I nod. "You'd think."

"Problem is some people just don't want to work." He stops for the traffic light. "Even my uncle has trouble with some of his employees."

"I thought they were all his church people."

Josiah chuckles. "Well, as you know, just because they're churchgoing people doesn't mean they're perfect. As my uncle likes to say, we're all just works in progress. The important thing is not to give up."

"Yes, that's true." For some reason this reminds me of my dad and his new living situation. Not that my dad would consider himself a churchgoing person anymore. Somehow I doubt that he and Selena will be attending church today. I just can't imagine the four of them stepping into a church.

"Is something wrong?" Josiah glances at me. "You seem quiet."

"Sorry. I was actually worrying about my dad just now."

"Is he sick?"

"Not exactly. Well, maybe he's sick in the head." And then I go ahead and tell Josiah about what my mom said. "I can't quite believe it. I mean, my dad used to be such a strong Christian. He used to talk to me about, well, all sorts of things." I almost mention how Dad used to encourage me to keep my purity pledge and save myself for marriage, but I can't bring myself to say that to Josiah. "Anyway, now my dad is . . . well, living in sin."

"Life's funny, isn't it?"

I just nod.

"But your dad has to live his own life. Just like you have to live yours. All you can do is keep making good decisions for yourself, Rachel." He grins. "And it looks to me like you're doing a great job of it too. If your dad's got any sense, he should be proud of you."

"I just hope I never make the same mistakes he's made." I sadly shake my head. "I'm so disappointed in him. Seriously, it's like everything feels upside down. Like I'm the parent and he's the kid."

Josiah chuckles. "I know what you mean. I reckon it's just part of growing up."

It's not long until we enter a gated road and Josiah informs me we're on his uncle's property.

"It's beautiful up here," I say as he drives past some fenced pastures where dozens of contented-looking cattle are peacefully grazing on lush green grass. "No wonder you guys make such delicious ice cream. Even your cows look happy."

"Uncle Jim takes the dairy business very seriously." Josiah pulls up to a big red barn with a sign on the front proclaiming *Lost Springs Dairy*.

"What a cool building," I say as he parks next to the blue-and-white delivery truck. "It reminds me of a children's picture book."

"If you like, we can start with a quick tour of the dairy. I'm sure you'll appreciate how well it's run."

I soon see that the old-fashioned exterior of the farm is not just a facade. While they do have a couple of automatic milking machines, there are also several people who are milking the cows by hand. And some workers are using old-fashioned devices that look like they've been around for a while. Meanwhile, others are operating modern-looking stainless-steel machines. It's all quite interesting.

It's also interesting to see there's some ethnic diversity here. Although the women look similar due to their long dresses, I notice a young Hispanic woman washing a cow. And I pause to watch a petite Asian girl as she wrestles with a butter churn.

"That looks like a good way to build up your biceps," I tell her. Looking up, she gives me a patient smile, then turns back to her churning.

"As you can see, my uncle likes both the old and the new," Josiah explains as he leads me past some freezers. "Originally, he wanted to do everything the old-fashioned way and without much reliance on outside electricity. But as his business grew, he had to get some new technology to keep up."

"Everything seems so clean," I say as we walk through a storage area. "I mean, considering it's a dairy farm."

"Some might think it's hokey, but my uncle is a firm believer that cleanliness is next to godliness." He chuckles as he leads me back out into the sunshine.

"Hey, that works for me. I wish your uncle could give my coworkers a lecture on the subject."

"Speaking of my uncle . . ." Josiah waves to a nice-looking middle-aged couple walking toward us. "Come over here and meet Rachel," he calls to them. After a quick introduction, I'm shaking hands with Reverend and Mrs. Davis. Like Josiah, they both have Australian accents. And they both seem very nice.

"Your dairy is amazing," I tell Reverend Jim. "Very impressive. I was already a fan of your ice cream. But seeing this place has won me over."

"Rachel works at Nadine's Natural Ice Cream Parlor," Josiah explains.

"So is this a field trip?" Reverend Jim asks me.

"Not exactly."

"Rachel came out here to try our church," Josiah tells him.

"Oh, you're the girl I spoke with on the phone," Mrs. Davis says. "Now I remember."

"Well, I hope you enjoy the service. It won't start until ten. But I'm sure Josiah will make you feel at home."

"I'm just showing her around," Josiah tells them.

"It's such a beautiful property," I say. "Such a lovely location for a dairy."

"And not a bad place to live either," she tells me.

"We'll see you later." Reverend Jim nods. And now Josiah and I continue with our walking tour. He shows me some more buildings related to the dairy. And then we walk down a wooded trail that follows the creek until we reach an area with lots of small wooden cabins nestled among the evergreens. There must be at least twenty of them.

"What is this? Some kind of a summer camp?"

"Lost Springs used to be a fishing resort," he explains. "The fly-fishing on the creek is exceptional, and fishermen would rent the cabins."

"It looks like some of them are occupied now." I notice a young woman hanging laundry behind one of the cabins.

"Yeah, some of the dairy workers live here." He points to a cabin off to our left. "That one's mine."

"How interesting and quaint. Do you live here year-round?"

"Sure. It's a bit rustic, but we've been insulating them so they stay warmer in the winter."

"I'd love to see inside of one," I say.

"I'd show you my cabin, but my uncle has strict rules about not entertaining the opposite sex . . . if you know what I mean."

My cheeks warm. "Of course. I wasn't hinting for you to invite me into your cabin, Josiah. I simply meant they look charming and I —"

"Just pulling your leg. Come on, I'll show you a vacant cabin over here. Who knows, maybe you'll want to move in."

He opens the door to reveal a small, dark interior where everything is made of wood. Wood-paneled walls, wood floors, and wood bunks. Enough for four to sleep. "Is there a bathroom?" I ask.

"You bet." He opens a door next to an open closet, revealing a tiny bathroom, complete with a shower. "All the comforts."

"Not bad." And although I don't mention it, I think this setup is preferable to the dorm where I live. At least it's more private here.

After we leave the cabin area, Josiah takes the creek trail, which eventually wraps around, bringing us to another open area and several more camplike buildings, all with brown wooden siding and green metal roofs. Only these structures are much larger than the cabins. And some of them look newer.

He points to a tall lodgelike structure with big double doors in front. "That's the meeting hall, where we have church." Now he points out an older-looking low building. "That's the dining hall." Finally he points to what looks like a well-made log house. "And that's my uncle's home."

"Nice." I nod with appreciation. "It all has such a good feeling to it. Everything is so orderly and neat." I look at the flower beds, with white and red petunias growing in straight, even rows. "Even the flowers are tidy."

He smiles. "Uncle Jim likes it that way."

"Well, I think it's all very lovely. It's like another country or going back in time. And not like the resort where I work either. They try to make everything look old-fashioned and sweet, but beneath the veneer it's rather disappointing." I smile at Josiah. "This feels real."

"How about a real cup of coffee or something cool to drink?" He leads me over to the dining hall. "Breakfast is over by now, but there are still beverages to be had."

I help myself to iced tea and Josiah fixes himself a coffee. "My mother would frown upon this too." He holds up the cup.

"Coffee?"

"GEF opposes caffeine as much as alcohol and drugs."

I nod. "That's right. It's one of the don'ts."

"Part of a long monotonous list. Fortunately Uncle Jim did away with that part too. We're allowed to drink coffee. But alcohol and drugs are still taboo."

I'm curious to hear more, but before I can ask, some young people come up to say hello to Josiah. As he introduces me, I focus on trying to remember their names. Sometimes I use a game my dad taught me to help remember people's names. You pick out something unique about a person and tie it to his or her name. However, these people strike me as strangely similar to each other. Not only do the women all have long hair, similar to mine, but they are also wearing longish dresses, which make my skirt look even shorter in contrast. However, everyone is warm and friendly and welcoming, and I don't feel too out of place.

"I reckon we better get over to church." Josiah points to the clock above the stone fireplace.

"Reverend Jim doesn't tolerate tardiness," a girl quietly tells me. "He says it's rude and insulting to be late."

"I completely agree." I remember how many times Belinda has insulted me by being rudely late to work.

We walk together as a group toward the tall meeting house. The double doors are opened wide, and I can hear music wafting out. For some reason I assume it's a recording, but as we go inside, I realize there's a small choir of men and women up in front. The singing is actually live. And it's very pleasant sounding too.

I smile at Josiah as he guides me up to one of the front pews. Although this building looks recently built, these wooden pews seem old. As we slide in, Josiah tells me in hushed tones that they were recycled from an old church. "I think they were from someplace back east. Like Pennsylvania."

"Very cool," I whisper.

Then as we sit there, quietly listening to the choir, I look at the big window up high in the arched point of the roof. It's just a plain glass window, probably about five feet by five feet. But with the tall evergreen trees and the clear blue sky and golden sunlight pouring through, it's far more exquisite than stained glass.

And suddenly, as I'm looking up there, I experience this unexplainable rush of joy—like God is really, truly here. Like he is most definitely in this incredible, amazing place—and I'm so happy I can actually feel tears filling my eyes.

I glance over at Josiah, wondering if he's experiencing the same flood of emotions. But his eyes are closed and his head is bowed as if he's praying. And that's when I notice everyone else's head is bowed in a similar fashion.

So even though I'd rather just stare out the beautiful window, I follow suit and bow my head as well. And with the clear, sweet tones of the choir's singing washing over me, I feel more spiritually alive than I have ever felt before. I feel like I am finally home.

"Someone's in a good mood," Belinda says in a slightly snotty tone as I'm humming to myself while scrubbing down the blender, which someone neglected to clean after making a triple berry smoothie that splashed all over the place.

"I'd be in a good mood too if I didn't come in to work until one and got to leave at six thirty," Lorna says.

"I wasn't even scheduled to work today," I remind them. "I only came in because Nadine was worried you guys would be swamped." And we have been swamped. In fact, this is the first time without a customer since I got here, and it's close to six thirty now. I'm well aware my coworkers are jealous that I have a short shift today. Even when I point out that they're getting time and a half for more hours, they're still mad at me. I suspect it's related to my sanitation seminar last night. But I wish they'd just get over it.

"I've been here since eleven," Belinda complains. "I should be the one getting off now."

"You should've asked me to trade with you yesterday," I tell her as I dip the washrag into the bleach solution and wring it out. "I already made plans for tonight."

I don't tell them that my plans involve going to church again. They wouldn't get it. They already teased me for going to church this morning. They'd probably really let me have it for going twice in one day. But when I heard that Reverend Jim has an evening service at seven, I felt desperate to go. To that purpose I actually packed my clothes from this morning and at exactly six thirty, I duck into Nadine's office, lock the door, and do a quick change.

Then I dash out the back door, avoiding more comments from my coworkers. As soon as I'm walking down the alley, I call my mom's number. To my relief, she doesn't answer. "I just want to let you know I'm going to church tonight," I say lightly. "I know you and Nadine are barbecuing burgers, but don't wait for me. I'm not sure if I'll be back in time to watch the fireworks. If I miss it, I'll see you tomorrow." Now I remember that I forgot to recharge my phone today. "And I'm not sure if this old phone has much charge left in it, so I'll probably turn it off. Have a good Fourth. Later." I'm just closing the phone as I reach the appointed meeting spot in front of the post office, where Josiah is already waiting for me.

"I hope we won't be late," I say as I hop into the small car. "I came as fast as I could."

"No worries. I explained the work situation to my uncle," he says as he takes off. "He was glad you want to come back and said not to be concerned about it. If we're late, we'll just slip in a side door and hopefully no one will notice."

"Thanks so much for picking me up." I stuff my work uniform deeper into my bag. "I know I already gushed about how much I like your church. But I really do appreciate you making the effort to give me a ride."

He gives me a genuine smile. "It's my pleasure, Rachel."

I look down at my skirt, which for some reason feels even shorter now than it did this morning. "I wish I had something more suitable to wear. I couldn't help but notice how the women at your church dress pretty modestly."

He nods in a halfhearted way. "Yeah . . . that's something my uncle insists on. I actually think it might've been Celeste's idea to start with. I'm not really sure."

"Is it a rule?"

He shrugs. "I don't know if it's a rule exactly. I just know that all the women dress like that. To be honest, I thought it was sort of odd at first. It took some getting used to, but now I hardly notice it anymore."

I tug the hem of my skirt down to my knees. "I kind of get it. I mean, it's aggravating that most girls don't practice any kind of modesty, so I think it's refreshing when women aren't flaunting their flesh." I giggle nervously. "I hate the uniforms Nadine makes us wear at work. Seriously, the first time I put on those short-shorts, I was like—*Are you kidding?* But then I suppose I got used to it. And with no air-conditioning, well, who wants to wear long pants? But when I think of how the women at your church were dressed today, well, it makes my uniform seem pretty skanky."

"I reckon I can see your point. But to be honest, I sort of fancy your work uniform." He laughs. "Of course, I won't admit that to my uncle anytime soon."

I gently punch him in the arm. "I guess you can't help that you're a normal hot-blooded guy. But the more I think about it, the more I understand why your uncle wants women to dress modestly. It just seems more proper . . . more dignified."

"So you wouldn't have a problem dressing like that?" He glances at me with a curious expression. "Wearing granny dresses?"

"That's what you call them?"

"It's what I thought when I first got here and saw all these women wearing baggy dresses down past their knees. It reminded me of my great-grandma back when I was a little tyke. She dressed just like that. Granny dresses."

"You know, as weird as it sounds, I think it'd actually be a relief to dress like that," I admit. "But I'm pretty old-fashioned at heart. To be honest, there's a lot about our culture I'm not real crazy about." Now I remember the scantily clad women I see in the ice cream shop all the time. Sure, they've been out on the lake, but I sometimes feel embarrassed or even disgusted by how much skin they're showing. "Seriously, when did it become acceptable for girls to go around practically naked?"

"It's been like that for as long as I can remember." He sighs. "But I lived in Sydney." He lets out a low whistle. "Believe me, you can see everything and anything on a Sydney beach."

"I'll bet you can." Now I feel slightly unsure. Does he disagree with his uncle on this issue? And if so, why? But just as I'm trying to think of a tactful way to ask him about this, he pulls over — right on the shoulder of the highway.

"What's wrong?" I ask as he comes to a fast stop.

He puts the car in reverse now, and with his head turned around, he quickly backs up.

"Where are you going — ?"

"A hitchhiker," he tells me.

"You're picking up a hitchhiker?" I give him a horrified look. Is he nuts?

"Uh-huh."

I turn around to see who he's going back for and am surprised to spot a young woman about twenty yards back. And speaking of scantily clad — or were we? — this girl has on shorts even skimpier than my work uniform. This is paired with a strapless purple band that looks more like a scarf than a top. To complete her ensemble, which seriously resembles a hooker, she has on tall shiny black boots. "You're really picking her up?" I say in a meek voice. "What if she's dangerous?"

He chuckles. "You think she's got a derringer in her boot?"

"Maybe . . ."

"It'll be all right. God is watching out for us, Rachel. And remember this morning's sermon? About how God wants us to reach out to everyone and anyone, no matter what they look like?"

"But . . . I . . . uh . . ." I don't even know what to say. I'm tempted to tell him my mom has made me swear to never pick up a hitchhiker. Never, ever. But then I'm not driving.

"G'day." Josiah sticks his head out the window, waving to her. "Come on — if you want a lift."

The girl walks up and bends down to peer in my window, and seemingly satisfied that we don't look like thugs, she climbs into the back of the small car. "Thanks for stopping! I was ready to give up."

"Where ya headed?" Josiah asks as he takes off.

"I don't really care. Maybe Seattle."

"You don't have any bags," I point out. "Traveling rather light, aren't you?"

"I had to make a quick getaway, if you get my drift."

"Well, it's doubtful you'll make it to Seattle tonight," Josiah tells her. "And hitching in the dark seems a bit dodgy."

"Are you British?" she asks. "I love your accent."

"Australian. Thanks. We happen to be on our way to church just now. If you want to come along, we can get you something to eat and a place to sleep for the night. Then you might have a better chance of catching a lift in the morning."

"Are you for real?" she asks in a skeptical tone.

"Sure," he tells her.

I turn around in my seat to get a better look. And when I see her face, I realize she's probably about my age and although she's trying to act confident, she seems a little uneasy. She's also got a lot of tattoos.

"I'm Rachel. That's Josiah. And yes, we're for real." Then trying to put her at ease, I start prattling away about how he picked me up from work and how I went to his church for my first time that morning. Then I describe what the place looks like and the dairy and even how I work at the ice cream shop at Rock Canyon Lake.

"You mean Nadine's?" she asks.

"Yeah." I nod. "Have you been there?"

"My parents used to take us there when we were kids."

"So, do you have a name?" I ask.

"Monique. I won't tell you my last name because it'd be a phony one anyway."

"Nice to meet you, Monique." I'm tempted to ask how old she is, but I sense she might not appreciate being interrogated. Besides she might simply lie about it. Girls do that . . . sometimes.

"So if you'd like some food and a bed for the night, you can come with us," Josiah says when we're a mile or so from the turnoff. "Otherwise, I'll just leave you here to catch another lift. Although I wouldn't advise it. A girl alone at night seems like an invitation to trouble."

There's a long silence and then she blows out a slow, loud sigh. "Okay, fine. You've convinced me. I guess I can trust you two—you seem relatively harmless. And I am exhausted and hungry. So if your offer of food and a bed is for real, sure, I'll take you up on it."

"Great." Josiah nods. "But first we go to church."

She groans. "Oh, man. Me in church . . . this is gonna be good."

"It's not like some churches," I assure her. "You might be surprised."

Of course, it seems that it's the congregation who should be surprised, I'm thinking as the three of us slip in a side door. Josiah with two girls in tow — one who looks like a hooker and one wearing a short skirt. Not to mention, we're late. To my relief, no one really seems to notice or care.

Once again, I'm pulled in with the singing and the general spiritual feeling of this place. And while I'll admit that I don't get all of the sermon's points and there are some parts I totally don't understand, there's so much I like about this place and about Reverend Jim that I don't really care. I figure it'll sink in better with time. And I plan to spend as much time as possible here.

When the sermon ends, Josiah asks if I mind sticking around long enough to get Monique something to eat and settled in. And I assure him that's no problem.

"What did you think of church?" I ask her as we walk over to the dining hall.

"It was better than I expected," she says as Josiah opens the door for us. "I guess I was pleasantly surprised." As we go into the kitchen, she explains about how her family never went to church. "The last time I was in a church, I was about twelve. I went with my best friend, and her preacher screamed and shouted at everyone. It was horrible. I never went back."

"Can't blame you for that." Josiah opens the fridge, foraging for food.

"But this seemed different," she says when he hands her an apple. "It made me feel kind of hopeful. Like there might be some reason to be alive."

"Sure there is." He spoons some potato salad onto a plate, adding some slices of ham and cheese. "Is this okay?" He hands the plate to her.

"Yummy." She nods eagerly, taking it over to a nearby table.

Now he looks at me. "I didn't ask if you were hungry, but I'll bet you haven't had dinner either."

I smile hopefully.

"Plate number two coming right up," he tells me.

As we sit there eating in the big dining room, Jim and Celeste come in and Josiah introduces them to Monique, explaining how we picked her up on the road. Jim studies the strangely dressed girl, and I'm curious as to whether his disapproval of her attire will show. But he simply smiles. "I hope you feel right at home during your visit. Welcome." Now he turns to Josiah. "Why don't you put her in with Lucinda Jones for the night? They have a spare bunk in their cabin."

Josiah nods.

I take another tentative bite of the potato salad. Now I realize that beggars shouldn't be choosy, but this potato salad is awful. Too much mayo and the potatoes aren't even fully cooked. Not that I'm complaining.

"If you girls want some dessert, there are several kinds of ice cream in the freezer," Celeste tells us.

"Ice cream?" Monique's darkly lined eyes light up.

"We make it right here at the dairy," Celeste tells her. "It's what Rachel sells at the resort." Jim and Celeste tell us good night, remind Josiah to lock up, then leave.

After we finish, we clean up after ourselves, and Josiah carefully locks the doors. "I guess someone started sneaking into the kitchen at night. So my uncle started locking it up."

"Can't blame him for that," Monique says. "With ice cream that good, I'd probably steal some myself."

It's getting dusky as we take Monique over to the cabins. I'm not sure if it was because of tonight's message or the food, but she's suddenly opening up, telling us about how she got in a fight with her boyfriend and took off. "He's a total jerk," she says angrily. "I gave up college in order to support him and his stupid band. And then I find out he's been sleeping with another girl the whole time." She swings her fist. "I walked in on them today. And then I walked out."

"That's gotta be rough," Josiah tells her.

"Do you have family or friends around here?" I ask.

"No. My parents used to live in Lewiston. But they moved to Spokane a few years ago."

We're just coming into the cabin clearing now. It looks cozier than ever with warm golden light pouring out from the square paned windows. And although it's not cold tonight, I can smell wood smoke coming out of one of the chimneys.

"This is it up here." Josiah steps up to the door of a cabin and knocks. This one is located on the opposite side of where his is, and a heavyset woman with long sandy hair opens the door.

"Hello, Josiah. How are you this evening?"

He introduces her to us and then explains about Monique's need for a place to crash. "My uncle said you might have a spare bunk for her to use tonight. Do you mind?"

Lucinda smiles and nods. "We'd love to have her." She hugs Monique, who looks shocked by this unexpected display of affection. "Welcome to our humble home."

"Thanks, Lucinda." Josiah waves to them and steps back. "I better get going. Gotta get Rachel back to the resort."

I tell Monique and Lucinda good-bye, and then Josiah and I trek back toward the car in the dark. But now I feel guilty as I realize Josiah is responsible for getting me home and then he still has to drive all the way back here.

"I'm sorry you get stuck driving me back and forth. I mean, it just occurred to me that it's an hour each time you make the round-trip. You'll have made it four times by the end of the day." I sigh. "That's a lot of driving."

He nods slowly. "Yeah, you're right . . . it's a lot of driving."

Now I don't know what to say. "I wish there was a bus or shuttle or something, coming out here from the resort."

"Don't misunderstand," he says quickly. "I don't mind getting you at all. I mean, sure, it's a lot of driving. But you're worth it, Rachel." He opens the car door for me with a sincere-looking smile. "I just wish you lived a bit closer."

"Me too." I slip into the passenger seat. "Maybe I can figure out a way to borrow a car," I say as he starts to drive away. "Anyway, I suppose I have a week to figure it out. Since there won't be church again until Sunday."

"Actually, we have a midweek service too," he tells me. "Wednesday nights at seven."

"Oh . . ."

"And then we have study groups during the week. To be a member of the church, my uncle expects you to commit to attend one of those as well."

Now I feel truly dismayed. "I suppose it's not very realistic to think I'm going to ever be a real member of this church."

"I reckon it's a big commitment, Rachel. It does take a fair amount of time. You'd have to want it really bad."

"I do want it really bad. I can't even explain how important it is to me. It's like, for the first time in a long time—maybe even the first time ever — I feel like I actually belong somewhere. It probably sounds weird to say, especially after such a short amount of time, but this feels like home."

"Truly?" He sounds doubtful. "You can tell that already?"

"I can. I just wish it wasn't so far out of the way. Or that I had my own wheels. I hate thinking I'm dependent on you to get me here, Josiah."

"If you really want to come, I don't mind getting you. I actually like driving. I mean, all day long I'm making dairy deliveries and it's fun. I like being on the road."

"You honestly don't mind?"

"Not at all. And my uncle probably won't mind either. Not if he believes you're really committed to his church. He only wants people who are fully committed."

"I'm fully committed," I reassure him. "I really, truly am."

CHAPTER 7

Seeing that fireworks are exploding over the lake when we reach the resort, I ask Josiah to take me over to Nadine's condo. This will allow me to spend some time with my mom before she leaves tomorrow. Instead of just dropping me off, Josiah parks the car and walks me up the condo stairs. But halfway up, the display above us is so spectacular, we both stop on the landing and just stare in wonder.

"Isn't it beautiful?" I say as a huge red, white, and blue starburst lights the entire sky, reflecting over the smooth black surface of the lake.

He nods, slips his arm around my waist, and pulls me closer to him. "It's almost as beautiful as you are, Rachel."

I feel myself melting inside as I turn to face him. Is this for real? And then he leans in and kisses me—several times and with an intense passion that takes my breath away. As we stand there kissing, I feel like I'm floating . . . like we're both floating. More dazzling explosions are going off up in the sky now, but nothing like the fireworks going off inside of me. This is a Fourth of July I will never forget!

"Sorry." He steps back and lets me go. "I didn't mean to get carried away like that."

I smile at him. "That's okay."

He nods with an uneasy expression. "Maybe . . . but my uncle would definitely not approve."

"Oh." Now I step back too. "Sorry then."

His lips curve into a smile. "Don't be too sorry."

I giggle. "Actually, I'm not."

"Just don't tell my uncle."

"You can count on that."

"Now I better let you go join your mother and your boss—before someone spies us down here."

"That's probably a good idea." I sigh happily. "Thanks for everything, Josiah."

"Thank you!" he calls as he turns and skips down the stairs.

Thanks to an opened bottle of wine, my mother and Nadine are both giggly and happy, and neither of them seems overly concerned or curious as to where I've been. But then why should they be since they think I was at church? And I was at church.

"The fireworks are really amazing." I sit with them on the terrace that overlooks the lake.

"You made it just in time," Nadine says. "I think they're about to have the grand finale."

I smile to myself as we watch more explosions, thinking I already experienced the grand finale . . . when Josiah kissed me. No fireworks, no matter how fantastic, could ever compare to that.

"You probably need a ride back to your dorm now," my mom says sleepily. "Since you work in the morning."

I point at the empty bottle of wine. "But you've been drinking."

She frowns. "Well, that's true . . . but not enough to—"

"Why don't you just let Rachel take your car," Nadine suggests.

Mom's not too sure, but we both talk her into it, and before long, I'm parking in the lot a couple blocks from the dorm. As I'm getting out and locking the car, I hear a girl's voice. "I didn't know you had a car."

I turn to see Steffie coming toward me. "Oh, hi. It's not really my — "

"If I'd known you had a car, I mighta been nicer to you." She laughs like this is amusing.

"It's actually my mom's car." I turn toward the dorm, but Steffie seems to be walking with me now. Actually she's staggering, and a few steps behind. "Have you been drinking?" I slow down, waiting for her to catch up.

"Jus' a little," she says in a slurred voice. "Jus' celebratin' the new year."

"It's not New Year's," I point out.

"Oh . . . I mean . . . well, you *know* what I mean."

"Independence Day?"

"Tha's right." She holds up a fist. "My independench day."

For some reason this makes me laugh. "Yeah, whatever."

Now she waves a finger at me. "Now you tell me somethin', Rashel. You tell me . . . who was that handshum guy the other night? The guy who looks like . . . oh, you know, that vampire dude. *Edward!* Who is that Edward you were with? I wanna know."

Considering her condition tonight, I'm surprised she even remembers that night at Frederico's. And I'm tempted to just blow her off now, but I stop myself. Maybe it's because of Reverend Jim's sermon or maybe it's because of how Josiah reached out to Monique, but I decide to be nice to Steffie.

I even catch her arm, steadying her before she stumbles on the boardwalk.

"That handsome guy happens to be my boyfriend," I say proudly. And I don't even think it's a stretch to say that anymore. Of course he's my boyfriend. We've gone out; he's kissed me. If that's not a boyfriend, what is?

"So you have a car *and* a boyfriend?" She shakes her head slowly. "Who wudda known?"

Instead of trying to straighten her out on the car, I tell her a little bit about Josiah. And although it's lame, I kind of enjoy talking to someone about him. What girl doesn't want to tell another girl that she's fallen in love? "His name is Josiah," I say in a dreamy way. "And I was with him tonight."

"Tonight?"

"Yes. For the whole evening. And we kissed during the fireworks and it was amazing."

She giggles. "Sounds like a real hot date."

"It was."

"Does Edward work here?" She pauses beneath a streetlamp to adjust her purse, moving it to the other shoulder as if in slow motion.

"His name is really Josiah." I wonder why I even bother. "No, he doesn't work here. But he delivers ice cream to Nadine's. He works at Lost Springs Dairy. They make natural ice cream."

"Los' Springs Dairy?" Her forehead creases like she's trying hard to think. "Isn't that . . . that freaky place?"

"Freaky place?"

She vigorously nods her head. "Yeah. Tha's it. Buncha freaky people with a freaky dairy. Los' Springs . . . tha's what it's called."

"Well, I've been there," I tell her as I open the door. "And it's not the least bit freaky. In fact, it's really cool."

Now she shakes her head. "No way. It's a freaky place. My friend went there and she said never again."

"What are you talking about?"

"Los' Springs. Aren't you lishenin' to me?"

"I think you've had too much to drink." I aim her toward her bunk and help her lie down. "Sleep it off and hopefully you won't feel too lousy in the morning."

"Goo'night." She closes her eyes.

I reach down and slip off her shoes, then drop them on the floor by her bed. I consider covering her with a blanket, except it's pretty warm in here and she's still dressed. "Good night, Steffie. Sleep tight. Don't let the bedbugs bite."

I hear her chuckling as I walk away. However, I doubt she'll feel very amused in the morning.

· · · · · · · · · ·

Monday is nearly as busy as Sunday. And while I try to be positive and upbeat and I'm basically in a good mood and working hard, it seems that my coworkers are determined to treat me like the enemy. Even when I tell Lorna that she's doing a better job cleaning out the machines at night, she acts like I've insulted her. I cannot figure out why they are so hostile toward me. Finally I just decide to do my work and interact with them as little as possible.

My mom stops by during my lunch break, and we get gyros to eat down by the water. It's finally cooling off some, only hitting the eighties today.

"I need to tell you something," my mom says in a tone that sounds serious.

"What? Is something wrong?"

"Not exactly." She sighs and takes a long sip of her soda. "It's just that we're probably losing the house."

"Losing the house?" I stare at her. "Our home? What do you mean?"

"I mean, the bank is foreclosing on us, Rachel. We got behind on house payments when Dad lost his job. I've never been able to catch up. And it's under water."

"Under water?" I imagine a flood sweeping over the only home I've ever known.

"Your dad got a second mortgage on it about eight years ago. It seemed like a good idea at the time, but now we owe more on it than it's worth."

"What are we going to do?"

"I found a place to rent," she says sadly. "It's kind of like where Nadine lives. You know those condos over on Napa Boulevard? Not too far from the high school?"

"Seriously?" Some of my friends call that area "the ghetto." That's where I'm going to live during my senior year?

"They have a fitness center and a pool. Plus it's closer to my work."

"We're going to live there?"

She makes a forced smile. "It won't be so bad. And it's just temporary, until I can find something better."

"When do we move?" I ask meekly.

"Don't you worry about that. I'll take care of everything. We'll be all set up long before school starts. I've already put a deposit on it."

"Oh . . ." I take a bite, slowly chewing, trying to process this.

"Anyway, I'm so glad you're in such a great place," she says cheerfully. "It makes this a whole lot easier."

"Huh?" I'm unclear on what she means. I do feel like I'm in a great place, at least I did . . . until now. But I haven't even told her about Josiah yet. How would she know what kind of a place I'm in? "What?"

"This resort, silly. What a great place. You're fortunate to have this opportunity, honey."

"Oh." I nod, taking a slow sip of my soda.

"I would've loved to have done this when I was your age." She sighs. "I wouldn't mind doing it now."

"You want to live here? At the resort?"

She wrinkles her nose. "Don't worry. I'm not going to move here. I'm just saying it's a fun place for a summer. You're lucky."

I shrug, trying to decide how much to say. Do I tell her I hate working at Nadine's? That my coworkers are beastly? Do I tell her that I have an Australian boyfriend who's almost twenty? No . . . sometimes ignorance truly is bliss. Besides, my mom's got enough to deal with. Her husband's left her for a younger woman and now she's losing our house. She definitely does not need to hear all the details of my life.

"This really is a pretty place." I look out over the smooth blue surface of the lake. "I am lucky."

Mom and I finish our lunch, then I walk her back to her car and we hug and say good-bye. But before she goes, I tell her not to feel bad about losing our house. "It's just a material thing," I say lightly, recalling what Reverend Jim said on Sunday. "God doesn't want us to obsess over possessions. He wants us to give everything we have to him—and then to trust him to provide for us."

She looks slightly surprised. "That's true, Rachel. I guess I need to keep that in mind. Thanks for the reminder."

I nod. "I heard it in church yesterday."

She pats me on the cheek. "Sounds like a good church."

"It is." I wave as she gets in the car and drives away. Then I go back to work, bracing myself for more frostiness from my coworkers and wondering if I should mention something to Nadine. Of course, since she's in the shop, they all act more normal and civil to me. So I simply put in my time, and to my relief Nadine stays later than usual. By the time my shift ends, I almost wonder if my coworkers have turned a corner.

However it's back to normal on Tuesday. Belinda comes late and acts like it's no big deal. Alistair comes on time and, as usual, seems to be eating out of Belinda's hand. I'm pretty sure he has a crush on her, and although I doubt she returns his affections, she has no scruples about utilizing them. But I comfort myself with the fact that since it's Tuesday and we're back to a normal schedule, Lorna won't be here until six, which means only thirty minutes in her unpleasant presence. So I'm caught off guard when Lorna arrives at three.

"Nadine is sick today," she tells us. "She asked me to come in early."

"She didn't call," I say.

"Are you questioning me?" Lorna glares at me as she ties on her apron.

"No, of course not." I shake my head. "I was just saying."

"Isn't it time for your lunch break?" she asks in an exasperated tone.

Without answering, I untie my apron, trying not to react to her rudeness as she turns to help the next customer. I cannot get out of there quickly enough. As soon as I'm out the door, I'm walking fast. I wish I could just keep going. I hate working at Nadine's. I hate working with Lorna and Belinda . . . and Alistair, too.

"Dear God," I pray as I walk, "help me." It's not much of a prayer, but it is heartfelt. I reach in my pocket for my phone now, tempted to call Josiah and complain to him. But he's busy making deliveries today. He stopped by the ice cream parlor to deliver some fresh cartons. We talked briefly but he seemed distracted. Besides, he was already running late and had to keep moving. I wish today were Wednesday. At least I'd have the midweek service to look forward to.

Today I go to Frank's Frankfurters and get a bratwurst, smother it in mustard, onions, and relish, then walk down to the lake to eat it. It's only in the high seventies today, so I'm not the least bit tempted to jump in the lake. But I do walk the trail a ways. I hope it will clear my head and prepare me for the next few hours of working with my disagreeable coworkers.

To my surprise, they all act fairly nice and normal when I return. Everyone seems to be working happily, and Belinda even offers to let me take over the cash register while she uses the restroom.

"One double scoop dish," I say as I ring up the next customer. "And one kid's cone too?"

"Plus a regular cone," he corrects. "That one already made it out the door."

I tell him the total and he hands me a twenty, but when I open the till, I'm surprised to see there's only two one-dollar bills, no fives, and one ten. "I'm sorry. We're out of small bills." I frown over at Lorna, who's dipping for some teen boys. Alistair is scrubbing down the food prep counter. I look back at the man. "Do you happen to have a ten?"

He looks in his wallet, then hands me his debit card instead. "Use this."

"Sorry about that," I say as I run the card.

"It's okay." He smiles as he signs the receipt. "I get perks with that card anyway."

"How can we be out of small bills?" I ask Belinda when she comes back.

"Lots of people came in with fifties and we've even had some hundred dollar bills." She shrugs. "Just one of those days."

"Well, someone needs to run to the bank to get some change," I tell her.

She shrugs again. "Guess so." But instead of offering to do this, she goes over to the waffle-dish maker and pours in some batter.

"Fine." I untie my apron and toss it beneath the counter. Then I grab four fifties and stuff them into my shorts pocket. "I'll do it myself."

No one even responds. It's like they're deaf and dumb . . . or zombies. Or maybe I'm invisible. I slam the till closed and stomp out of there. Seriously, what is wrong with them?

It takes me about thirty minutes to go to the bank, wait in line, watch as the teller counts out the bills and slips them into a white envelope, then I walk back to Nadine's. By the time I open the door, I've recovered from being mad.

"Hey there," Lorna says in a surprisingly friendly tone. She's standing by the door, almost as if she was waiting for me. Before I can respond, she snatches the bank envelope from my hand. "I'll take that. And not a moment too soon either." She hurries over to where Belinda and Alistair are huddled by the register. "We already lost a couple of customers while you were gone." She hands the envelope to Belinda.

"What took you so long?" Belinda demands.

"There was a long line at the bank." Now I go over, curious as to why they're all huddled around the register like that. "What's going on?"

Belinda closes the till and then turns, giving me a puzzled look. "What do you mean?"

Just then a loud group of teenybopper girls comes in, and since none of my ditzy coworkers seems inclined to go take their orders, I grab my apron and a scoop and wonder why I'd even bother to try to figure these three out. The good news is, I have less than two hours left to work.

Finally my shift ends and I slowly walk back to my dorm. I wish I had somewhere more interesting to go, but the truth is, I'm almost too tired to really care. The past few days have been good but exhausting. All I want to do is take a nice, long nap. As I'm drifting to sleep, I remind myself that tomorrow is Wednesday. After my shift ends, Josiah will pick me up to take me to the midweek service . . . and life will be good again.

When I get to work on Wednesday morning, I'm surprised to discover that the lights are already on as I'm unlocking the front door. Did Lorna forget to — I stop in my steps. Someone is already in the ice cream shop.

"Who is it?" I call without going inside. Is this a break-in? In broad daylight? With pounding heart, I'm ready to make a fast run.

"Rachel?" I hear what sounds like Nadine's voice calling.

"Nadine?" I cautiously go in. "Is that you?"

"In here," she calls from the office.

"What are you — ?" I stop myself when I see that both Belinda and Lorna are in there with her. All three of them are looking at me with impossible-to-read expressions. "What's going on?" I ask.

"That's what I'd like to know." Nadine's voice sounds hoarse, but then I remember she's been sick.

"Huh?" I peer at her, trying to figure this out.

"Lorna reported money missing from the till last night."

"What?" I turn to Lorna, but she gives me a completely blank look.

"When she was closing last night . . ." Nadine speaks slowly, like it's difficult. "She was balancing out . . . and the till was two hundred dollars short." Nadine narrows her eyes slightly.

"*What?*" I hold up my hands, confused. "I still don't get this."

"I counted it too," she tells me. "She's right. Two hundred dollars is missing."

"But what does that have to do with me?"

She points to her laptop now. "The girls suggested I download the surveillance video from yesterday. So I did." Now she clicks her mouse and I see a black-and-white scratchy-looking image appear on her screen. I lean forward, squinting to see, and I realize it's the interior of the ice cream shop. I can see the end of the ice cream case, the cash register, and part of the yogurt machine. Belinda is at the register and it looks like business as usual. She's making change, smiling. The customer leaves, and then Belinda moves away from the register area and out of the camera's view.

A moment passes and then I see myself, dressed in my uniform and adjusting my apron. I go to the register and soon I'm waiting on a middle-aged man with a dish of ice cream in his hand. Of course, there's no sound, but I watch myself having a conversation with him, and eventually he hands me his card. I ring up his purchase and give him a receipt.

He leaves and now I'm looking all around with an odd expression. Kind of a mixture of confusion and irritation. I look to the left and to the right. And although my lips are moving, it's silent. And then I get this really aggravated look on my face, and I reach into the till and grab out some bills and shove them in my pocket. I slam the till shut and walk away. I blink and turn to Nadine. "I realize that looks bad, but it's not what it seems."

She gazes at me with a sad expression. "You, of all people, Rachel. I never thought you'd steal from me. Never."

"I didn't steal." Now I explain how we were out of change.

"Out of change?" She looks extremely skeptical. "That's very unusual. In all the years I've run this place, I don't think I've ever run short on change. And Lorna assured me she'd left lots of change in the cash bag the night before."

"And you saw how many small bills were in the cash bag this morning," Lorna tells her. "How could we have possibly run out?"

"That's because —"

"Do you deny that you removed two hundred dollars from the till?" Nadine asks in a tired tone.

"No. I did take two hundred dollars, but I —"

"That's all I need to hear." She stands now, putting a hand to her forehead. "I have a fever of 102 degrees. I really should be in bed."

"But I didn't take —"

"I *saw* the tape, Rachel." She glares at me. "A picture is worth a thousand words. I just wish I'd never had to see it. And for a mere two hundred dollars. Really? I would press criminal charges except your mother is my friend . . . and I'm too tired."

"But I put the money back."

"The money is gone, Rachel. I saw you take it on the tape. I've heard Lorna and Belinda's testimony. There is nothing more to say. I am going home."

"Except that I didn't —"

"Give me your keys." She holds out her hand. "I mean *my* keys."

I dig the keys out of my pocket and drop them in her hand. "You're wrong about this, Nadine."

"Just leave — now!" Her voice cracks. "Before I call the police."

"Take it easy, Aunt Nadine," Belinda says gently, helping Nadine sit back down. "You'll make yourself even sicker."

"See what you've done?" Lorna hisses at me.

"But you have to listen to me, Nadine," I insist. "I didn't do—"

"Leave her alone!" Belinda tells me. "Can't you see she's not well?"

"Why don't you just go?" Lorna points to the door. "You are not wanted here."

"But I—"

"Just go!" Belinda yells at me. "Stop torturing my aunt like this."

"I'll send your final check to your home," Nadine tells me in a tired tone. "Minus the two hundred dollars you stole from me."

"But I didn't—"

"Oh, *Rachel*!" She sadly shakes her head. "I am not well enough to argue with you. Can't you see that?"

"Just go," Belinda firmly tells me. "Don't make this any worse than it is."

My hands are shaking and my head is throbbing. I'm so upset that I feel like I could actually throw up. And all three of them glare at me with such judgment and hostility and contempt that I know it's useless. Their minds are made up. I am guilty. I simply turn and walk out.

Hot tears rush down my cheeks as I head back toward the dorm. This is so unjust, so unfair, so wrong. But how can I get her to listen to me? How can I prove that I've been framed? Because that's what happened. Belinda and Lorna put together some diabolical plan to get rid of me. I just know it. Instead of going into my dorm, I turn and walk down to the lake. As I walk, I try to replay everything that happened yesterday. Finally, I think I know exactly what they did.

Someone snuck the small bills out of the till while I was on my lunch break. Because Nadine was home sick, it was their perfect opportunity. The plan was to trick me into thinking we needed change. Belinda let me take over the cash register so I discovered we were short. Naturally, no one offered to do it. So, as usual, I took matters into my own hands and grabbed the big bills and ran off to the bank.

Now I even understand why the three of them were clustered around the register like that. It must've been their way to conceal what they were doing from the camera they knew was running. I suspect if I went over the whole tape, I could point these things out to Nadine. But would that be enough to prove I've been framed?

Even if she would listen to me, how would I explain the missing two hundred dollars? Money that Lorna and Belinda must've pocketed by now. Those lying thieves! It would be their word against mine. Two against one. And Belinda is Nadine's own flesh and blood. Who's Nadine going to believe? I'm guessing that even if Alistair is aware of what happened, naturally he would side with Belinda and Lorna. Three against one.

I sit on a bench and, burying my head in my hands, start to cry. Why has this happened? What did I do to deserve this? All I tried to do was be a good worker. And this is where it gets me. I consider calling my mom, but I don't even know what to tell her . . . or how to say it. And suddenly I'm worried. What if she doesn't believe me? What if Nadine tells her about the tape and the missing money and my mom takes her story over mine? Besides that, I think about my mom's disappointments over my dad and losing our house — how will she feel hearing that I've lost my job as well? A job she felt I was so fortunate to have, so lucky.

All this is bad enough, but now I'm aware of something far more disturbing. Something that makes me cry even harder. I'm suddenly aware that with no job here at the resort, I won't be able to afford to stay on at the dorm. I will have to go home. And if I have to go home, I'll be three hours away from Josiah. It will be a deathblow to our relationship.

So now I wonder about the chances of finding a different job here. There are lots of restaurant and hotel jobs. Although this is only the middle of the season, already some people are being laid off. I would even be a dishwasher if it was a way to stay on here, to continue spending time with Josiah. But then I have to ask myself, without good references from Nadine, which is so not going to happen, who would hire me?

In desperation I pull out my phone, and without thinking of what I'm going to say, I dial Josiah's number. Waiting for it to ring, the lump in my throat grows so big that I'm not even sure I can speak. By the time he says "Hello," I'm crying harder than ever. "Josiah," I gasp.

"Rachel?" His voice is filled with concern. "What on earth is wrong?"

"Everything!" I sob. "My world is falling apart. I don't know what to do."

"Where are you now?"

"Down by the lake," I gasp. "By the gazebo."

"I'm not far from the resort. Stay put. I'll be there in about fifteen minutes."

I thank him, then close my phone. Taking in some long deep breaths, I attempt to control my emotions, wipe the tears from my cheeks, and finally get my wits about me. I begin to pray. "God, help me," I whisper. "Help me to figure out this mess. Please help."

Before long, Josiah is down by the lake with me. Of course, seeing him and the compassionate look on his face undoes me and I start to cry again. Between choked sobs, I pour out my strange and twisted tale, and poor Josiah, dressed in his crisp white shirt and pants, wraps me in his arms, assuring me that it's going to be all right. "God has bigger plans for you. Somehow this is going to turn into something better."

"I don't see how," I say sadly.

"No, of course you don't. You're in the midst of it right now."

I nod, wiping my nose with the back of my hand and feeling like a mess. "I . . . I don't know what to do. With no job, I'll have to go home now."

"Do you want to go home?"

I shake my head no. "And my mom won't be happy to hear she has to pick me up. She doesn't even get off work until after five. And it's almost six hours for the round-trip. Plus she was just here." I sigh. "And now I'll miss church tonight, just when I really need it too."

"Maybe you should stick around," he suggests.

"Yeah . . . my rent in the dorm is paid to the end of the week."

"Or you could come stay at Lost Springs, if you want."

"Seriously? I could stay there?"

"Sure." He pushes a strand of hair away from my face. "Did I tell you Monique decided to stay on?"

I blink. "Monique? She's still there?"

He nods, then chuckles. "Believe it or not, she's working in the dairy now—with the cows. And she actually likes it."

I try to imagine Monique in her shorty-shorts and tube top and tattoos . . . milking a cow. It just doesn't make sense. "You're kidding, right?"

"Not at all. She and Lucinda really hit it off. And you should see Monique in a granny dress. You wouldn't even recognize her."

"Seriously?"

"Anyway, I don't want to pressure you. And I should get back to making deliveries. But if you're interested, I know I can talk Uncle Jim into letting you stay with us. If you're willing to work. No one can stay more than a day without working."

"I don't mind working at all," I assure him. "I think that's what messed things up at Nadine's. Belinda and Lorna resented how hard I worked. It made them look bad."

"Well, that won't be a problem with us. Hard work is rewarded at Lost Springs."

Now I consider how it will feel to remain here at the resort with no job and nothing much to do until the weekend. Hanging at the dismal dorm is not appealing. "I'd love to come stay at Lost Springs," I tell him suddenly. "And I'm happy to work. At least until the weekend. Until my mom can pick me up."

"Great!" He grins as he takes my hand, pulling me to my feet. "How soon can you be ready to go?"

"As long as it takes me to pack. Like fifteen minutes?"

"Perfect."

We plan to meet in fifteen minutes in front of the dorm. And going our separate ways, I suddenly realize that I'm no longer upset. Instead I feel excited and happy and am looking forward to this new opportunity. I've heard of "blessings in disguise," but I'm not sure I've ever experienced one. However, I'm sure that's what this is. What Belinda and Lorna intended for bad has turned into something totally good.

It reminds me of *The Sound of Music*—one of my favorite movies, which I've seen dozens of times—the part where Maria remembers what Mother Superior told her, how when God closes a door he opens a window. As I stuff my clothes into my bags, I feel like that's exactly what's happening to me.

As I strip off the detested pink-and-white uniform and shove it into my bag, I am tempted to break into singing, *"What will this day be like?"* because I realize now that the door to Nadine's has been slammed closed and locked tight, never to be walked through again.

But I don't even care. In fact, I'm relieved. Because the beautiful window to Lost Springs is wide open to me, and I'm happily climbing through it. As I pull on my jeans and a T-shirt, gather up my bags, sling straps over my shoulders, and hurry out to meet Josiah, I feel like my life is about to begin!

CHAPTER 9

"You really don't mind riding with me while I finish making deliveries?" Josiah asks me again.

"Not at all. It's actually kind of fun to see what you do."

"Great. I know our customers will appreciate getting their orders."

As I ride along with Josiah, I'm amazed that what started out as the worst day of my life has turned into one of the best days I can remember. I even help him carry in some of his deliveries. And in between stops, we talk or sing along to the radio. I'm almost disappointed when we finish the last one.

"I'm starved," he tells me as he's driving us back to Lost Springs. "They've already had lunch, but we can still raid the fridge."

"I'm hungry too." I start feeling a little nervous as he goes through the security gate. What if his uncle doesn't approve of this? What if I have to return to the dorm?

"You all right?" he asks.

"Uh, yeah . . . sure."

"You look uneasy."

"I was just wondering what I'll do if your uncle doesn't want me to stay." I look out at the happy cows, grazing in the sunshine.

"Why wouldn't he want you to stay?"

I look back at him and shrug. "I don't know . . . maybe I'm still recovering from what happened this morning at Nadine's."

"Of course he'll want you to stay, Rachel." But now he frowns. "Except I should warn you about something."

"What's that?"

"Well, Uncle Jim is very firm about how men and women should and should not interact with each other, if you know what I mean."

"Not exactly."

"Well, remember when we stopped to, uh, to watch the fireworks?"

I can't help but giggle. "Yeah . . ."

"Well, that would not be acceptable here at Lost Springs."

"Oh." I nod. "I get that."

He sighs. "Good."

Now I feel a little confused. "So how should I act then? I mean, when I'm around you?"

"Like we're brother and sister."

"Right . . . brother and sister."

"I know. It seems a little hokey. But Uncle Jim is pretty conservative about some things. And I reckon it's best not to rock the boat with him."

I consider this. "It must be a challenge to run a big place like this. I mean, it's like your uncle is in charge of everything and everyone—not just the dairy business, but the church too. That's a big responsibility. I can understand why he wants people to respect his rules."

"As long as you understand that, you should do all right here."

He's parking by the big red barn now. I help him unload the empty crates and clean out the back of the truck, and then we go over to the dining hall where a large redheaded woman warmly greets Josiah but eyes me with suspicion.

"Eleanor, this is Rachel. She'll be staying with us for a while." Josiah grins at the older woman. "Eleanor is the head cook and kitchen boss. She sees to it that everyone is well fed here."

"Pleasure to meet you." I smile at Eleanor, remembering the tasteless potato salad from the other night and wondering if that was her handiwork. Naturally, I will not express my opinions on the cuisine.

"We have leftover pasta salad and roast beef," she tells us as she turns to check something she's mixing in an industrial mixer. "Help yourselves, but don't leave a mess, you hear?"

"Yes, ma'am." Josiah makes a mock salute behind her back as he leads me to the oversized refrigerator. Before long, we both have plates of food. To my disappointment, the pasta salad is really just macaroni with dressing and nearly as bland as the potato salad from the night before. Fortunately, there is salt . . . and the roast beef is better. Still, I can't help but wonder about Eleanor's cooking skills.

"Did you go to culinary school?" I ask her as Josiah and I are cleaning up after our lunch.

"Oh no, of course not." She waves her hand in a dismissive way. "I learned how to cook from my mama back when I was just a girl. I've been cooking ever since." Now she gives me her résumé by listing all the places she's worked. Not surprisingly, they're all institutional establishments, school and hospital cafeterias. "I was head chef at Pleasant Valley Nursing Home for ten years before I came to work here for Reverend Jim."

I nod, trying to act impressed.

"Rachel has dreams of owning her own restaurant someday," Josiah tells Eleanor.

"Really?" She frowns at me. "That's a mighty high aspiration. Do you honestly believe that's what God has planned for you?"

I glance uneasily at Josiah, wishing he hadn't told her about this. "I . . . uh . . . I'm not sure. I guess I never thought of it like that."

"Then maybe you should." She turns back to the mixer, scraping down the sides with a rubber spatula. "It's no use chasing a foolish dream if the good Lord isn't the one giving you the dream. Remember, God's ways are higher than man's ways."

"I'll keep that in mind." I exchange a glance with Josiah. He's just grinning like he thinks this is a good joke on me.

"Rachel has some experience with cooking," he continues talking to Eleanor. "And since she's going to be here a few days, I wonder if you'd like her to give you a hand here in the kitchen."

Eleanor turns back around and studies me. "You think you can handle working in a kitchen like this? Taking orders from me?"

"Sure." I nod. "I know how to take orders."

She looks up at the clock. "Are you ready to go to work now?"

"I want to get her moved into a cabin first," Josiah says. "And I need to talk to my uncle to be sure he approves."

She looks surprised. "Well, yes, of course. I wouldn't want her in here helping me without the reverend's approval. First things first."

"How about if you expect her to come to work for you tomorrow?" Josiah suggests. "That'll give her a chance to settle in."

"Yes, yes, that'll be fine. Now you kids run along. I got plenty to do before suppertime."

We tell her good-bye and head down a path that appears to be going to where he said his uncle lives. But instead of going up to the big log house, he takes us down another path that leads around the house. And to my surprise, there are even more buildings back here. Six houselike structures are arranged in a semicircle with a large shared grassy area in front. "What are all these?" I ask.

"Homes," he says.

"Who lives in them?"

"They're the deacons' houses." Now he points to another building, off to one side. "And that's my uncle's office."

"This place is bigger than I realized. How many people live here?"

He presses his lips together like he's thinking. "I'm not sure. I reckon it's around a hundred . . . or more."

"Wow, I didn't realize."

He opens the door to the office, and a buzzer sounds as we go into what looks like a reception area with a large desk on one end and a couch and some chairs, like a waiting area, on the other.

"Hello, Josiah." A pretty young woman emerges through a doorway behind the big desk. Dressed in the usual granny dress, although it looks a bit more stylish on her, she smoothes her long honey blonde hair as she sits in the office chair, smiling up at us.

"Hello, Rose." Josiah politely introduces us.

"Nice to meet you, Rachel." She turns back to Josiah. "Now what can I do for you today?"

"Is Reverend Jim around?"

She opens up what looks like a date book, and picking up a pen, she appears to be studying it, almost as if she's not sure herself. "Yes. He is in today. Do you have an appointment?"

"No, I didn't have time to make one. Is he pretty busy?"

She picks up a phone receiver now. "Let me find out for you."

We wait as she announces to him that Josiah and a friend are here to see him, then hangs up. "Please, have a seat and the reverend will be with you in a few minutes."

Josiah thanks her and we go over to sit down. I'm thinking the reverend must be pretty busy not to be able to see his own nephew without an appointment, but I don't say anything. I don't want to appear disrespectful.

About ten minutes pass before Rose answers the phone and proceeds to announce that the reverend will see us now. "Go on in, Josiah," she tells him.

He leads me through another door and down a short, dimly lit hallway where he knocks on a dark wooden door.

"Come in, Josiah."

He opens the door, waiting for me to go in first. Reverend Jim is seated at a massive wooden desk, with a window to his back so he's framed in light. "Hello again, Rachel. Please sit down. Both of you. Wednesday afternoons are usually reserved for prayer and meditation . . . in preparation for the evening service."

"Sorry to pop in on you like this," Josiah tells him as we settle in the chairs opposite his desk. "But it is imperative that I speak to you, Uncle Jim."

The reverend leans forward now, peering curiously at both of us with troubled dark eyes. "This sounds serious. Is something wrong?"

"No," Josiah assures him. "Not wrong exactly. It's just that Rachel needs a job and a place to live. So I brought her here. I hope that's all right."

Without responding, the reverend looks intently at me, almost as if he's trying to discover my motives or see into my soul. I feel my cheeks flushing and I wonder if this is a mistake.

"I told Rachel that we could accommodate her," Josiah

presses on. "And I think Eleanor would like her to help out in the kitchen. Rachel has some experience with that sort of thing. I mean, if it's all right with you."

Now the reverend fixes his gaze on Josiah. "So is that all this is? Rachel is simply looking for work and a place to live? Nothing *more*?"

"Certainly, she's interested in our way of life here. She's hungry for what you teach at church." He glances at me. "Right?"

I nod eagerly. "Yes. Absolutely."

"And that is *all*?" The reverend's gaze moves from Josiah to me and back to Josiah again . . . waiting.

Josiah looks uneasy now. "Yes, of course that's all. What else would it be?"

Now the reverend actually begins to chuckle. "I'm sorry, but for some reason I thought you brought her in here to announce that you two wanted to get married." He laughs louder.

"Married?" I can't help but gasp. "Seriously?"

Josiah just laughs with his uncle, as if that was a pretty good joke. I can't help but feel slightly offended by this. I'm not even sure why exactly. Is it because of what the reverend assumed or because Josiah thinks it's so funny?

The reverend looks back at me now. "How old are you, Rachel?"

I'm still stuck on the marriage thing . . . as well as trying to decide how to answer. If I admit I'm seventeen, he might make me leave. On the other hand, it feels wrong to lie to a man of God.

"She's eighteen," Josiah says for me.

"I'm sorry," the reverend tells me. "I can see that I caught you off guard with my assumption. But as you get to know me better — and I hope that you will — you'll come to appreciate that I call it as I see it. And for some reason I got the impression that Josiah and you were here for *another* reason."

He pauses, quietly watching me as if he's still not convinced we're not secretly planning to elope. Naturally this makes me nervous. Because, sure, I do like Josiah—perhaps I even love him—but marriage? *Seriously?*

"Rachel's had a rough day," Josiah says. And now I'm taken aback as he proceeds to tell him about what happened at Nadine's. It's not that I don't want the reverend to know about it, but it's unsettling hearing it again.

"So you're truly innocent?" the reverend asks me.

I nod. "I honestly am completely innocent. I was totally blindsided by my coworkers." I sigh. "Although in hindsight, I should've seen it coming." And now he asks me to explain, so I tell him the whole ugly story.

"Why do you think your coworkers treated you this way?" he asks.

So I tell him about how I'd been concerned about sanitation and how I had higher work standards.

"She made them look bad," Josiah adds. "They resented it."

Now the reverend smiles and nods. "Well, as they persecuted our Lord unjustly, so they will persecute us. You should be honored, Rachel."

"Honored?"

"It's an honor to be persecuted for righteousness' sake."

"Oh." I nod. "Yes, I do remember reading that in the Bible before."

"Are you familiar with the Bible?"

I tell him a bit about my church history. He asks me a few theological-sounding questions and I do my best to answer, finally admitting that I'm not as well versed in the Bible as I wish.

"No worries," he tells me. "That is why we're here. We will all learn together." He looks at Josiah. "I think Rachel will be comfortable in Miriam's cabin."

Josiah looks surprised. "Miriam?"

The reverend puts the tips of his fingers together, almost in a praying posture, and nods. "Yes, Miriam's influence will be just what Rachel needs." He smiles at me. "Rachel is a good name. I have a very good feeling about you."

For some reason this gives me great hope. "Thank you! And thank you for letting me stay here. I promise to work hard."

He nods. "I believe you will."

"We'll let you get back to preparing for the evening service." Josiah stands and the two of them shake hands.

"Tell Miriam I'm counting on her to make Rachel feel right at home here," Reverend Jim says. "If she has any questions, she can come speak to me."

Josiah nods. "I'll do that."

Before we leave, I thank the reverend for welcoming me like this. "I already told Josiah, but I felt right at home the first time I came here."

"That's a good sign, Rachel."

Walking back to the delivery truck, where my bags are still stashed, I feel a wonderful sense of excitement—as if I'm embarking on a big adventure. I chatter away as we carry my stuff over to the cabin area, but then I notice several young women walking together, and I'm suddenly reminded of how my wardrobe doesn't exactly fit in here.

"What about my clothes?" I glance down at my jeans and cringe at how grungy and out of place I look. Even Josiah, still wearing his delivery uniform, looks much nicer and neater than I do. "Will that be a problem?"

"I'm sure Miriam can help you figure that out," he tells me. But something about the tone of his voice sounds different. Almost as if he's not sure about this now. Is he questioning whether or not I can fit in here? Second-guessing himself for bringing me?

I hold my head high. I will do all I can to convince him that this is not a mistake. I will make him and his uncle proud of me. I can do this. I will do this!

"Miriam works in the dairy," Josiah explains as we walk. "But her shift should be over by now. Hopefully we'll find her at home." He pauses, glancing over his shoulder almost as if to see if anyone is watching us. But the three girls have gone into one of the cabins now. "I need to tell you something," he says in a hushed tone.

"Is something wrong?"

"Not exactly. You just need to know that Miriam is . . . well, she can be a bit cranky if you know what I mean."

"A bit cranky?" I can't help but smile at this.

"Don't get me wrong; Miriam is quite devout, but she can be a bit negative and harsh at times. And I don't want her to drag you down, Rachel. You have such a good spirit." He reaches his hand out as if he wants to touch my face but then draws it back as if someone could be spying on us. "Don't let Miriam change that."

I nod, trying to absorb all this. "Thank you, Josiah. I'll keep that in mind." I give him a confident smile. "And don't worry. I'm pretty tough. I mean, if you consider the abuse I took at Nadine's. Miriam can't be any worse than that, can she? I mean, this is a Christian environment."

He shrugs. "Yeah . . . you're probably right." Hoisting the strap of my biggest bag more securely over his other shoulder, he nods over to where a tall, thin woman is stepping outside of one of the cabins. "Speak of the devil," he says, almost under his breath.

"What?"

"Just joking." He chuckles. "Sorry 'bout that. I know my uncle wouldn't see the humor in that." He waves toward the woman with his free hand. "Miriam. Someone I want you to meet over here."

As we walk toward Miriam, I'm suddenly reminded of someone but I can't quite recall who. Then as Josiah introduces us, I get it—with her dark, beady eyes and long, narrow nose, Miriam reminds me of the Wicked Witch of the West in *The Wizard of Oz*. Even her brown hair that's streaked with gray has a slightly witchlike look. But then she smiles and, grasping my hand, warmly greets me and—poof—the silly witch image completely vanishes.

"I've seen you around and about here," she says in a sweet voice, which also has an Australian accent. "I've been hoping to meet you."

"Rachel is going to be with us for a while. My uncle suggested she might be able to stay with you. Do you mind?"

"If Reverend Jim thinks it's a good idea, so do I." She reaches for one of my bags, taking it from Josiah. "I've been feeling a bit lonely since Kellie and Brandy left."

Josiah seems to bristle at something, glancing at me with a furrowed brow as she reaches for the second bag. "Yes . . . I suppose you're ready for a new roommate."

"Come on," she says to me. "Let's get you settled in. I'm sure you already know that there are no guests here. If you're part of this community, you're expected to work. If you don't work, you don't eat."

"I'm aware of this," I assure her. "I actually like to work."

"Then you're in the right place." She slaps me on the back. "Now come on."

I glance back to see Josiah still standing there with what seems like a perplexed expression. For the second time I'm worried that he thinks I won't be able to cut the mustard here. And so I give him a confident wave and a broad smile. "See you later," I call out as Miriam leads me into her cabin.

"These cabins look so cozy." I look around the sparsely furnished room. There are four bunks, each topped with a handmade quilt. There are four small three-drawer pine dressers, four small pine desks, and four wooden chairs. On the floor is a large braided rug in a rainbow of colors. "Did someone make that?"

Miriam nods. "I did. It's a way to recycle unneeded clothing."

"It's pretty."

"Thank you." She points to a bed in the far corner. "That's my bed there. You can select any of the others."

I set one of my bags on the bed by the only window. "This one will be fine."

"That window can be drafty. You might want to switch come winter. That is if you're still here by then. Josiah didn't say how long you intend to stay."

Now I feel uneasy. Will they be as friendly and accommodating to me if they know I only plan to be here for the summer? Now that I think about it, nothing was said about the duration of my stay. If they consider me just a visitor, will I be treated differently? Will I even be welcome? Should I pretend that I'm considering staying here indefinitely?

"How long do you intend on staying?" she presses.

I smile and shrug. "I guess I'm not really sure. This is all so new to me. I'm still sort of adjusting to everything."

She returns my smile. "And there's no need for me to pressure you. After all, we live one day at a time around here. Tomorrow will take care of itself."

"Yes." I nod eagerly. "I believe that too."

Miriam's lips form a tight line and her dark brows draw together. "However, even if you're only here for just a day, if you plan to work and be part of our community . . ." She points to my jeans. "Those will not do at all." She shakes her head. "Not at all. The Bible makes it clear that women are not to dress like men. And we take that seriously here."

"I apologize for my appearance. And I'm aware that I need to wear a dress. Unfortunately, the only dresses I have aren't very long."

She makes a tsk-tsk sound. "That's simply the way of the world, is it not? Women going around dressed like men or like harlots and not thinking a thing of it. Goodness, when I saw Monique on Sunday — oh my! Thankfully, she was agreeable to burning her clothes."

"She burned her clothes?"

Miriam looks startled. "Certainly." Now she points to her rug. "Those horrid rags weren't even worthy of walking upon."

I nod. "I do remember being concerned when we picked her up on the highway that evening. I mean, judging by her clothes, she was a little scary."

"Thankfully, she has seen the error of her ways."

"That's really amazing." I smile, but the truth is, I'm still trying to wrap my head around this. I haven't actually talked to Monique yet. Not since Sunday anyway. But is it possible that she's really done a complete turnaround? Maybe miracles do still happen.

"Now, as to your wardrobe needs." Miriam bends down and pulls open one of the drawers on the dresser near her bed. "I realize I'm a bit taller than you, but perhaps we can make this work." She pulls out a long plain dress in a nondescript shade of dark blue and holds it up.

"Oh . . . ?" I study the drab dress, trying to imagine myself in it.

"Go ahead, put it on." She hands the dress to me.

Suddenly I feel self-conscious, not sure that I want to disrobe in front of this complete stranger. Of course, this is silly considering that I've been living in the dorm with women I never knew before, showering and dressing in front of them. However, there is something unsettling about being alone in here. "Do you mind if I change in the bathroom?"

She frowns. "Is there something you feel a need to hide?"

"No . . ." I shake my head. "I guess I'm just a little shy."

"All right. This time you can do that. But I don't want you to start using the bathroom as your private dressing room."

I sigh, not wanting to rub her the wrong way. "Okay then. I'll just change out here." But I turn my back to her as I remove my clothes. As I struggle to pull the dress over my head, I remember that I'm wearing some rather skimpy underwear. Not skimpy compared to what most girls wear, but I'm sure it's skimpy compared to what someone like Miriam must wear. Not that I want to think about that. Fortunately, she doesn't say anything.

I push my arms through the sleeves, arranging the bodice of the dress around my waist, then turn to look at her.

"It's a little long," she says. "But it won't be dragging in the dirt. If you want to shorten it a bit, I don't mind. I doubt I'll wear it again. Of course, you may not know how to sew." She rolls her eyes. "I'm appalled at how many girls arrive here and don't even know how to thread a needle. But that doesn't last for long. As a matter of fact, I teach the beginner's sewing classes. Would you like me to sign you up to join us on Thursday night?"

"I already know how to sew. I've been sewing since I was twelve."

She looks surprised. "Well, that's a skill that will be useful around here."

"And I can cook too." I stand taller, feeling thankful for all my years in 4-H.

"Goodness. Josiah did well to find you, didn't he?" But now she scowls. "But I do hope you won't let these skills give you a big head. We are all equals here. No matter how talented or pretty or smart—we show no preferences. It makes no difference. We are all equal and the same in the Lord's eyes."

"Yes, of course. I wasn't trying to brag." Okay, maybe I was.

"So since you won't be in the beginner's class, I will sign you up to attend our Saturday-night sewing circle." She points to the patchwork quilts. "We made all of those. And we make dresses and shirts and curtains and all sorts of good things."

"Yes, I'd like to be part of that."

"As for your cooking skills, perhaps you'll want to help in the kitchen."

I explain that we've already spoken to Eleanor about this very thing. "And Reverend Jim agrees that'll be a good place for me to work." I consider telling her about my dream of running a restaurant someday, but that might sound like I'm bragging again. I'll have to be careful about that.

"Do you mind if I use the restroom now? I mean, I really have to go."

She chuckles. "Well, of course. Go. You don't need to ask to use that, Rachel."

I notice three things about the Spartan bathroom: (1) there is no mirror above the sink, (2) the hand soap appears to be homemade and smells funny, and (3) the hand towel feels like cardboard. As I hang the stiff towel back on the wooden bar, I wonder if this was how the pioneers lived. When I return to the room, I find Miriam going through my bags.

"The reverend will expect me to show you what's acceptable here . . . and what is not." She points to a small pile on my bed. Only underwear and socks and my T-shirt nightie. Now she places my toothbrush and my hairbrush next to it. "That should do it." She zips up the bag and turns to me.

"You're kidding. What about my shampoo and—?"

"You'll find everything you need in the bathroom."

"So . . . what about my other things?" I point nervously at my bags. Hopefully she's not planning to burn them.

"That depends."

"On what?"

"On your level of commitment." She studies me closely.

"I'm not sure what that means."

"Yes, it takes some people longer to decide."

I just nod.

"In the meantime, we better get these things into storage." She picks up one of my smaller bags.

"Storage?"

"Don't worry, they'll be safe." She nods to the other bags. "Come on, let's get moving."

I gather up my bags, leaving my purse on my bed.

"Get that too," she tells me.

"But my cell phone is in there."

She laughs. "You won't be needing that."

"But I—"

"Didn't Josiah tell you that cell phones are not allowed?"

"But he has one."

"I'm sure he uses one for making deliveries. But I assure you that he doesn't have one for his personal use."

I'm not so sure, but I don't want to argue with her. Instead I pick up my bags and follow her outside. We walk over to a small building with no windows, and she unlocks a door and tosses my bag in there. "Go ahead and leave your other things here too. If you decide to leave, they'll be returned to you."

"Okay . . ." I feel uncertain as I set my bags in this small dark space, but I notice there are other bags and boxes and things stacked about.

"You'll be surprised at how much a person doesn't need," she tells me as she locks the door.

"I'm sure you're right. I've often said that everyone has too much stuff." As we walk back to the cabin, I feel strangely free and unencumbered. And suddenly I think I see the reasoning for this. Things really bog a person down.

In the cabin, Miriam sits down on her bed and sighs. "My dairy job is an early one. I rise and shine at four thirty."

"Four thirty in the morning?"

She laughs. "Well, certainly not in the afternoon." She looks at the small alarm clock on her dresser. "Otherwise I'm already late. As a result, I like to take a wee nap before dinner. Just a short one. So if you'll excuse me . . ."

"Certainly." I step back as she lies down. "Maybe I'll take a walk around the grounds."

"No, you won't." She sits up as if alarmed.

"Why not?"

"Women are not permitted to walk on the grounds unaccompanied."

"Oh . . ."

"Look in the top drawer of your dresser," she tells me sleepily. "You'll find something to read there. I suggest you start reading it."

I remove a paperback book with a curling cover that's been printed to resemble old parchment with the words *The Real Testament of Jesus Christ* printed across the top in large block letters, and below in smaller letters it says: *The Lost Springs Edition.*

I open the book to chapter 1 and begin to read what sounds faintly familiar . . . kind of like the Bible, yet different somehow. Not that I'm much of an expert on the Bible, but I have gone to church and attended youth group for most of my life. But now that I think about it, I never really learned too much about the Bible during those years. So as I slowly read the first few pages, I attempt to absorb the gist of the meaning. And I'm somewhat reassured that it sounds similar to what I heard Reverend Jim say in church. Still it's a little like wading through a swamp or hacking my way through a jungle. Like I want to scrape away half of the words to extract the real meaning.

But I persevere and by the time Miriam wakes, I think I'm grasping it . . . somewhat. Basically this book is saying that we live in a sinful generation that will soon be judged by God. And unless we change our wicked ways, we will experience the wrath of God in full force. But if we repent from our worldliness and gather ourselves together, waiting on the Lord with pure hearts and receiving godly instruction, we will be preserved from the wrath and condemnation that is coming. After that it gets murkier.

"I see you took my suggestion," Miriam says with approval. "Do you have any questions about what you've read so far?"

I consider this. "Well, I think I got most of it, although the last part was a little confusing."

"How is it confusing?" She stands and slips her dirty feet into a pair of black flats that are scuffed and worn down on the heels.

"The part about a last day's prophet who's supposed to lead his people to safety just like Moses led his people. Who is that?"

Miriam finger-combs her long gray-streaked hair. "Well, it's Reverend Jim, of course."

I try not to look too surprised. "Reverend Jim is a prophet?"

"Not *a* prophet, Rachel. He is God's *chosen prophet*." Now she's tightly braiding her hair into a long rope she secures with a rubber band, then flips over her shoulder.

"Oh . . . ?" I don't want to appear skeptical and I do think Reverend Jim is a gifted preacher. But God's chosen prophet? I'm not so sure about this. However, I think it might be wise not to express my real thoughts on this subject. After all, I've only heard him preach twice. And both times I got an unusual feeling inside.

"Doubt is of the devil," she proclaims, as if reading my mind. "If you wish to be part of this community, you must do battle with your devilish doubts." She points at the book still in my hand. "That is your sword, Rachel. Use it to slay your doubts."

As Miriam and I walk to the dining room together, my eyes are searching the grounds for Josiah. I feel the need to talk to him, to be reassured by him. But it's not until we're inside the dining hall that I spot him. When I wave at him, starting to go over to him, Miriam stops me by grabbing my arm.

"Women eat on *this* side of the room."

"Oh . . . ?" Again, I try not to look shocked.

"Men and families eat over there." She tips her head over to where Josiah is talking to a man I haven't met.

"I didn't know about that."

"Yes, well, I couldn't help but notice that you sat with Josiah both times you visited here for church service. That was the men and family side. I'm sure Reverend Jim overlooked this because you were a guest. But since you're no longer a guest, you will be expected to sit on the women's side."

I make a stiff nod, acting as if this makes sense.

Now her expression softens and she places a hand on my shoulder. "I know it's hard to understand these things when you're new. But you'll see that it's really for the best. It eliminates temptation and distraction, allowing us to focus on the teaching."

"I guess I can understand that," I admit. To be honest, I was somewhat distracted when I sat next to Josiah. There were moments when I was more aware of Josiah sitting next to me than I was of the reverend's preaching. Perhaps I'll absorb his teaching better without that kind of distraction. Still, I long to speak to Josiah. But now I'm afraid that will be forbidden as well.

Dinner is another disappointing meal of blasé foods prepared in a bland and boring way. As I poke at my pasty mashed potatoes, I wonder if there's a spiritual reason to have tasteless food. Perhaps it's sinful to enjoy eating. In that case, I may be in trouble because my love of food and flavors will be difficult to shake.

Miriam introduces me to several of her friends. They're all older than I am, and although they try to be pleasant, I find their conversation to be about as exciting as the menu.

After dinner, people are milling about in front of the dining hall, and to my relief, Josiah approaches me. "How's it going?"

"I don't know . . ." I glance over my shoulder.

"Something wrong?"

I shrug. "It's just not quite what I expected."

"I know there's a lot to get used to here."

"I didn't realize there was so much segregation."

"You mean separating men and women?"

I nod.

"Yeah, that takes some getting used to."

I force a smile. "But it's okay to talk to you like this now?"

"Sure. With other people around us like this, it's all right."

"But no private conversations?"

He shakes his head no.

"I'll miss you."

Now he smiles. "We might be able to find a way around this."

Feeling Miriam's gaze on me, I try not to look too hopeful. "How?"

"There are ways."

"I know you have a cell phone," I say. "But mine was confiscated."

"Phones are no use here. The cell phone I have is really for business use. But we can communicate in other ways. I'll figure something out."

"Speaking of phones" — I suddenly remember something — "I need to call my mom . . . or else she'll be worried. I mean, if she calls my cell phone and I don't answer or return her calls."

Josiah's mouth twists to one side. "Yes, you should definitely do that."

"How?"

"You can use the cell phone." He explains that it's in the delivery truck and that the truck is unlocked. "Go ahead and use it. Go right now, before it's time for the service to begin. If anyone sees you, just explain that I said it was all right. I'd go with you, but that would just attract more attention." He turns away and walks over to where a group of older men are talking.

Feeling like a criminal but seeing that Miriam is now visiting with her friends, I slip away and head directly for the dairy. As Josiah said, the truck is unlocked and the cell phone is right where he said it would be. Still feeling nervous, I dial the number to my house, but as it's ringing I think I should've dialed my mom's cell instead.

"Hello?" a man's voice says.

"Oh? I'm sorry, I must have the wrong number." I hang up and look to see if I dialed wrong. But the number in the call history is correct. Feeling curious, I dial it again. This time my mom answers. "Who was that?" I demand.

"Sorry," she says a bit breathlessly. "That was Tom. From my work. Do you remember him?"

"Why's he answering our phone?"

"He's helping me pack."

"Pack?"

"Yes. I'm moving us into that condo unit I told you about. Tom's saving my life by helping me."

"You're moving? Right now?"

"Yes, Rachel. I told you we're losing the house. If I don't pack up and get us out of here, we could lose our stuff as well."

"You're packing up my room too?"

"Actually Tom's doing that."

"Tom is packing up my room?" I can hear the anger in my voice. But seriously, why is a strange man going through my things?

"Don't go ballistic, Rachel. Tom has two daughters. It's not like he's never seen girl stuff before." She laughs like this is funny.

"*Mom!*"

"I'm tired and this has to be done. You're not here to help, and Tom is. I don't need you to throw a hissy fit."

Now I'm too mad to say anything.

"Look, Rachel, the good news is we'll be all moved by the weekend. Then I'll drive up there and get you, and you can get settled into your new room."

"That won't be necessary," I say crisply.

"Did you get another job?"

"Yes." I take in a deep breath and just hold it.

"Oh, that's wonderful. Good for you!"

Now I wonder if she's glad that I found another job or glad that I won't be coming home anytime soon.

"What kind of job?"

I let the breath go. "In a restaurant." I force brightness into my voice, trying to coat my lie like a sugar donut. "As a sous chef."

"Oh, Rachel, that's fantastic. I'm so happy for you."

I sigh. "Sorry I got so grumpy over Tom packing my room. I'm sure it must be overwhelming. That's nice he could help you."

"It is overwhelming, sweetheart. And sad. After living in this house all these years and now sorting it all out . . . overwhelming doesn't even begin to describe it."

"Do you want me to come home and help?" Suddenly I think this is the answer. My mom needs me. I should go.

"No. You stay put. With Tom's help, I'm making good progress. And it actually feels good to thin things out. Less is really more. Right?"

I think about my new Spartan lifestyle. "Yeah . . . I guess so." I see someone walking into the dairy and I duck down. "Well, I better go, Mom. And by the way, that old cell phone you gave me isn't working. I had to borrow a friend's phone to call you. But don't worry, if I need anything I'll call you from the, uh, from the restaurant. And I'll be pretty busy."

"You and me both, Rachel. Thanks for calling. Love you, honey!"

"Love you, Mom." I close the phone and take in a slow, calming breath. It doesn't feel good to have just lied to my mom. But I didn't know how to tell her where I really am or what I'm doing here. What am I doing here? Now I hear the sound of a bell ringing and I realize that must be for church. So, checking to be sure no one's around to see me, I slip out of the truck, quietly close the door, and jog back over to the meeting hall.

"Where have you been?" Miriam demands.

"I had to use the restroom."

"But there's one in the dining hall. You weren't there."

"There's a restroom in the dining hall?" I say innocently. "I guess I didn't need to go all the way back to the cabin then."

"Well, let's hurry. It won't do to be late."

As we file in, I notice that the left side is only occupied by females. Whereas the right side has a mix. Families fill the front five or six rows and then men—and not very many—fill the rows behind them. It's not like I want to take a head count tonight, but I'm somewhat surprised to see that women must outnumber men by at least four to one, and I can't help but wonder why.

The midweek evening service feels much more serious than the Sunday services. And as hard as I try to listen, I feel like I'm only able to take in bits and pieces. Much of what Reverend Jim says is similar to what I read this afternoon, but much of his theology goes way over my head too. And yet something about it is compelling and appealing. And it's reassuring to think that God has such a definite plan for order and discipline. Plus I find the reverend's focus on doing our best and the power of servitude to be refreshing as well as challenging. Especially after my recent experience at Nadine's, a place where no one seems to appreciate diligent workers.

It's getting dusky as people gather outside of the meeting house to visit. And once again, since this is a public place, Josiah approaches me, politely asking me if I liked the evening service.

"Very much so. I think this place is a much better fit than working at Nadine's."

He looks relieved to hear this.

"Speaking of Nadine's, I wondered if I could send my uniform with you the next time you make a delivery there."

"Sure. That will be Tuesday morning." He glances around to see if anyone is listening. "And I have an idea for communicating. You know the bench that's near the trail right before you turn off to the cabins?"

"Yes." I try to act natural, not like we're making some clandestine date, although that's what it feels like.

"I'll place a large stone right next to that bench, arranging it so a note can be slipped beneath it. Now if you walk by and see there's a pebble on top of the big stone, you'll know there's a note underneath." He smiles, glancing around again. "Make sense?"

"Sure. Sounds like a good plan."

"And here comes my uncle now."

"Hello." Reverend Jim smiles as he greets us. "Are you getting all settled in, Rachel?"

"Yes, Miriam has been very helpful."

His gaze skims over my drab dress. "I see she's assisted you with some, uh, appropriate attire." He looks at Josiah now and chuckles. "Although it appears that Miriam went out of her way to be sure it was one of the worst-looking dresses I've seen in this place."

Josiah laughs. "I was thinking the same thing, Uncle. Just didn't want to say it."

Feeling embarrassed, I smooth my hands over the skirt of my dress. "It's okay. It doesn't really matter."

Now Reverend Jim is waving over to his wife, motioning for her to join us. "You've met Celeste, haven't you?" he asks as the pretty blonde woman comes over and stands by him.

"Yes. We met last Sunday."

He grins at his wife. "I was just telling Rachel that her dress is one of the ugliest things I've seen in ages."

"Oh, Jim," she scolds in a humored tone. "What a thing to say."

"Well, it's true. Don't you reckon?"

Celeste gives me an apologetic smile, then sheepishly nods. "I'm sorry, Rachel, but I must agree with my husband on this."

"I know Miriam meant well," the reverend says to us, then turns to his wife, "but perhaps you could help Rachel find something a little less homely to wear."

"I certainly can," she tells him.

"Although we want our women dressed modestly and decently, we do not expect them to look like bag ladies."

"Jim." Celeste pokes him in the arm as she glances around to see if anyone else is listening or might be offended by this. "Go easy."

He laughs. "Rachel knows that I speak my mind. I call things as I see them."

I nod eagerly. "And I respect that. I really do."

Now he gets a serious expression. "I just hope you'll feel that way if I ever have to confront you on a difficult subject."

"I'm sure I will."

"Now as far as your wardrobe needs," Celeste says to me. "Why don't you stop by the house tomorrow morning and we'll see what we can do? Say, tenish?"

"Sure." I eagerly nod. "And I do know how to sew. I could probably make my own dresses if I had some fabric and could borrow a sewing machine."

"You can sew?" Celeste seems truly impressed by this. She turns to Josiah and gives him a sly smile. "You certainly found a good one, didn't you?"

Josiah lets out a nervous laugh. "Rachel is full of all sorts of hidden talents."

Celeste studies me with clear blue eyes. "I have a feeling you're a real treasure." She reaches out to clasp my hand in hers, giving it a warm squeeze. *"Welcome."*

Miriam comes over to join us now. "I reckon we should head back to the cabin," she tells me. "Your shift won't start as early as mine, but you have a busy day ahead of you all the same."

"That's right," Reverend Jim says. "Early to bed, early to rise makes a soul happy, healthy, and wise."

I know that's not exactly how that old Benjamin Franklin quote goes, but I know better than to correct him on it. Instead I tell everyone good night and walk with Miriam back to our cabin.

"The reverend seems to have taken a shine to you," she says as we go into the cabin.

Something about the way she says this feels a little unsteady to me. "I suppose that's because I'm Josiah's friend," I say lightly. "The reverend seems to care deeply for his nephew."

"The reverend is no respecter of persons," she says a bit sharply.

"What does that mean?"

"It means we are all equal, Rachel. No one is better than anyone else. Whoever would be great must learn to serve."

"That sounds right." Sitting down, I take off my sandals and let out a long yawn. "I'm so tired. And it's so incredibly quiet here. I'll bet I sleep like a baby tonight."

"Nothing compares to the sleep of the just. A clear conscience is better than the best sleeping pill."

I turn away as she begins peeling off her dress. Not so much out of respect, although that's certainly part of it, but more because the sight of her bony body and wrinkly skin makes me feel too uncomfortable.

CHAPTER 12

Because no one told me what time I'm supposed to report to work and because I slept so soundly, I don't show up at the dining hall until breakfast time. But as soon as I'm done eating, I go into the kitchen.

"I'm here to work, if you need me," I tell Eleanor.

She scowls at me. "It's about time."

"I'm sorry. But no one told me what time I was expected to come to work."

"Seeing that breakfast is at eight, I'd think you'd figure it out."

"I'm really sorry. I hope you can forgive me."

Now her face softens. "Yes, of course I can forgive you."

I reach for an apron, slip it over my head, and tie it behind me. "Now what time do you want me to come to work in the mornings?"

She pushes a damp strand of hair from her forehead and sighs. "Seven is early enough."

"Fine." I nod. "And what would you like me to do?"

She glances over to where a couple of girls are rinsing dishes and loading them into the sliding commercial dishwasher. "Bethany and Lydia, come here and meet Rachel."

The girls come over, wiping their damp hands on their aprons and looking shyly at me as we're introduced. I'm surprised to see they're even younger than I assumed. Probably a few years younger than I am.

"These girls are sisters," Eleanor explains. "Their father is Deacon Don. The girls usually work here in the mornings and do their schoolwork in the afternoons."

"Except during summer," Bethany clarifies. "We don't have school again until September."

"So we work full days," Lydia fills in.

"Well, I suppose it's still nice to have a break from the books." I almost admit to them that it's summer vacation for me too, but I don't want to even hint that I'm still in high school.

"Rachel is going to help with the cooking," Eleanor tells them.

"I hope to lighten Eleanor's load."

Bethany and Lydia seem to appreciate this as they return to the dishes, and I suspect they've been on the receiving end of Eleanor's bad moods from time to time.

"I have a couple other helpers too," Eleanor explains. "Marsha comes in at ten and works until eight. And Hannah is in charge of the chickens and the garden, and sometimes she helps out in the kitchen too."

"You have a garden?"

Eleanor nods as she picks up a clipboard, looking at what appears to be the week's menus. "And a greenhouse too. Our goal is to become completely self-sufficient for our food. No small task when you consider how many mouths we have to feed 'round here. Even so, we're getting close. There are only a few items I have to purchase from the outside world—ingredients like soda and salt and yeast. But I try to keep stocked up on those things."

She hangs the menu clipboard back on a nail. "Why don't you go out to the garden and tell Hannah that I need some onions for lunch."

"How many and what kind?"

Her brow creases. "Four or five white ones."

"Where's the garden?"

She points to the back door. "Go out there and follow the gravel trail. You'll find it. And take that compost bucket with you."

The gravel trail is bordered by a tall hedge and leads me for about fifty feet before it opens up into an enormous lush garden with tall wire fences around it. And there's a large greenhouse off to one side. I go through a gate into the garden and soon spot a brunette girl wearing a lilac-colored dress and wielding a hoe.

"Hello," I call to her. "Eleanor sent me out to get some onions."

"Hello." She comes over with a curious expression. "Who are you?"

I introduce myself and she tells me her name.

"Your garden is beautiful, Hannah."

She shakes her head. "No, it's not my garden."

"Well, you're the gardener and you must be doing a pretty good job because it's truly lovely."

She looks down at her bare feet and mumbles, "Thank you."

I hold up the bucket of smelly compost garbage. "Eleanor asked me to bring this to you."

She removes the bucket from my hand. "That goes over here. Do you want to see the compost pile?"

"Sure." I follow her over to what looks like a wooden pen full of dark brown dirt. It smells a little ripe but looks like rich soil. She tosses the contents of the bucket onto it and then rakes it through. "I also raise worms." She grins at me. "Some people are creeped out by that, but I think it's cool."

"How long have you been gardening?" I actually want to know how long she's been here but am worried that it's rude to ask.

"I've always wanted to grow things. But I've only been the gardener here for a couple of years." She leans the rake against a post and studies me. "I'd just turned eighteen when I first came here, but I didn't get to work in the garden that first summer. I had to prove myself worthy." Her lips curve into a partial smile. "But now I'm the head gardener and I have girls working for me."

I explain that I'll be helping Eleanor in the kitchen. "She seems a little overworked to me."

Hannah nods. "She is. That's great that you want to help cook." Now she frowns. "Just be careful."

"Careful?"

Hannah presses her lips together, almost as if she regrets her words.

"You mean of Eleanor's feelings?"

"Yes." She nods eagerly. "You wouldn't want to step on her toes."

"Right."

"The onions are over here." She leads me over to what looks like a garden shed. "I store root vegetables and onions and things in here." She opens the door and we go into a cool, dark area that smells of hay and vegetables. "How many do you need?"

After I've got the onions, she gives me a quick tour of the garden. I'm impressed with all the variety—everything from berries to kale. "So many great choices. This is like a chef's paradise."

"Yes . . . you'd think."

Now I remember the bland menu. "But Eleanor doesn't really utilize all these great foods, does she?"

Hannah's eyes light up. "Not like I wish she would. But maybe you can help her to try some new things."

"I'll see what I can do," I promise as we walk back to the gate.

"The chicken yard is right over there," she says.

"I thought I heard them." I peer over a wooden fence to see a large henhouse and a bunch of colorful-looking chickens scratching in the dirt.

"I have—I mean, we have Plymouth Rocks and Leghorns and Rhode Island Reds and Barred Rocks and Light Sussex." She holds up her hands. "And I'm probably forgetting someone."

"Sounds like you know your chickens."

Her smile comes more easily now. "I do. I've even given some of the best brooders names."

"Well, as interesting as this is, I should get back to the kitchen."

"Nice meeting you," she calls.

"You too," I call back. I really like Hannah. She seems real and down to earth. Okay, she's obviously very down to earth. But she seems like someone I could get to know better. Someone I'd like to know better.

"I got the tour of the garden and the chicken yard," I tell Eleanor as I go inside. "That's quite an operation. Something many cooks would dream of having."

"Yes, I suppose so." She pauses from measuring flour. "You can chop up those onions for me. I want real small pieces. Minced, if you know what I mean. The knives are over there by the stove."

I select a good-looking chef's knife, and before long I am chopping and blinking back tears. I dump the finely chopped onions into a bowl and take them to Eleanor. Glancing at the clock, I remember my appointment with Celeste. "I'll have to go for a bit just before ten," I tell her.

"What?" She turns and glares at me. "You've barely just got here and now you're running off? What for?"

So I explain about Celeste and she simply nods. "Well, of course. I wouldn't want you to miss that. When do you expect to be back?"

"I have no idea, but I can tell her that you're busy and that I need to —"

"No, no, don't do that. Just come back as soon as you're done. Hopefully you'll be of some use before lunch. We serve at twelve thirty."

"Yes, I'm sure I'll be back long before that. In the meantime what would you like me to do?"

She assigns me some more prepping tasks, and I do them all cheerfully and as quickly as my hands will safely move. But finally it's nearly ten and I'm washing my hands, trying to rid myself of the onion smell. I excuse myself, hang my apron on the peg by the door, and hurry on my way.

As I walk toward the big house where Jim and Celeste live, I smooth my hair, wishing that I had a mirror to check myself in, but no one probably cares what I look like. Well, except that Reverend Jim thought my dress was ugly last night. To be fair, it is ugly. But even so, I feel a bit confused. First Miriam tells me that appearances don't matter and then Reverend Jim seems to think they do. Which is it?

Feeling a bit nervous, I go up to the large front door and ring the doorbell, biting my lip as I wait. A pretty young woman with strawberry-blonde hair opens the door. "You must be Rachel," she says brightly. "I'm Kellie."

Now I know that Jim and Celeste have children because I've seen them at church services, but so far I haven't quite figured out their names and ages. "Are you one of the Davis kids?" I ask as she leads me inside.

She giggles. "No. And don't let Celeste hear you saying that." She lowers her voice. "She's not really old enough to be my mom."

"Sorry." I glance around the large foyer and am surprised to see that it's actually quite elegant. Unlike the more rustic exterior, this space has marble floors and a large antique-looking table with a big crystal vase of fresh flowers — with a mirror behind it. A real mirror. I try not to spy my own image, which I know must look pretty frowsy. "This is really pretty."

Kellie just nods, leading me past a curving staircase and down a hallway. "Celeste is back here." She pauses by a closed door, then taps lightly. "Rachel is here to see you."

"Come in," Celeste calls.

Kellie opens the door, motioning for me to go into what looks like a small living room. Like the foyer, this room looks elegant too. With hardwood floors, oriental carpets, and pretty furnishings, I feel caught off guard, like the interior of this house doesn't match the exterior. Maybe this is how Alice felt on the other side of the looking glass.

"You have a beautiful home," I tell Celeste as I go over to where she's sitting at a desk in front of a window that overlooks a beautifully landscaped backyard with a tall rock wall surrounding it.

"Thank you." She turns and smiles at me. "Because you are Josiah's special friend, I feel comfortable having you here. But you need to understand that not everyone here enjoys this privilege."

I nod, standing there and feeling homelier than ever in the presence of so much beauty. There are paintings on the wall, mostly landscapes, although one is a portrait of Celeste wearing a beautiful sky-blue gown with a surprisingly low-cut bodice.

"I can see you're shocked by how we live," she says in a weary tone.

"No, not shocked exactly . . . I'm just trying to take it all in."

"Well, as you must know by now, Jim is God's chosen prophet and God has also chosen to bless us." She waves her hand. "Far more than we ever expected. But then who are we to question God's blessings? He owns the cattle on a thousand hills. Why should he not give us whatever he pleases?" She smiles. "And for that we are truly grateful."

"Yes . . ." I don't know what to say, what to do, how to act.

"I'm sorry, please sit down, Rachel. I don't know why I'm rambling like this." She gets up from where she's sitting, moves to the sofa, and pats a spot next to her. "Sit, please."

I sit beside her, folding my hands in my lap. "Thank you for inviting me into your home."

"Yes, as I was saying, because of your relationship to Josiah, who is like a son to us, it seems only fitting that we bring you into our inner circle too. Josiah has assured us that we can trust you with our friendship."

"Of course. I have the utmost respect for you and Reverend Jim. And I'm so thankful you've welcomed me." It's funny when I talk like this; it feels like I'm someone else or playing a part in a movie.

Kellie returns with a tray. "Here's your tea," she tells Celeste and sets the tray on the table in front of the sofa. "Anything else?"

"No. Thank you, Kellie."

After she leaves and closes the door, Celeste pours us both a cup of tea, handing one to me. "Now, I realize you thought I was going to talk to you about your wardrobe, and we'll get to that. But first I wish to speak to you about Josiah. Both Jim and I can see he is attracted to you. And that you share the same feelings." She peers over her cup at me. "Am I correct?"

I feel my cheeks warming but simply nod.

"And that's not a problem. Because Josiah is our nephew, he is allowed some special privileges. For instance, if he chooses to marry, Jim will provide him with a home." She waves her hand. "Of course, it won't be as fine as this, but it will be suitable for a young couple."

I take a quick sip of tea, feeling it scalding my throat, and try not to cough and sputter as I set the teacup back into the saucer. Is she suggesting Josiah and I should get married?

"I can tell by your reaction that you're not ready for this, Rachel. But you need to understand that it's more honorable to marry than to burn."

"What?"

"It's more honorable to marry than to burn."

"I'm not sure I understand."

She smiles in a tolerant way. "We prefer that couples — certain couples who have obtained the blessing of the prophet — marry rather than be tempted to commit fornication. Now do you understand?"

While fornication isn't a part of my normal vocabulary, I do know the meaning. "But I would never consider having sex outside of marriage. I've even signed a purity pledge."

She looks relieved. "I told Jim you were a good girl. But as he pointed out, even a good girl can lose her way. He asked me to speak to you directly on this."

"But I wouldn't—"

"No matter." She waves her hand again. "I think I've made myself perfectly clear. Now let's talk about your wardrobe needs." She places a forefinger on her chin, then frowns at my dress. "Jim was right. That dress is appallingly ugly."

She stands. "Come with me." She leads me over to another door that goes directly into a very feminine-looking bedroom. "I realize you're more slender than I am, but we're about the same height. And if you're handy with a needle, I'm sure you can do some alterations."

"Yes, that's no problem."

"Good." She opens another door and flips on a switch that illuminates a spacious walk-in closet. "Come on in here and we'll see what we can find."

I try not to gape at the surprisingly large space, but I think it's nearly as big as the cabin I'm sharing with Miriam.

"Here." She hands me a floral print dress. "This is a little too young for me." Now she hands me a robin's egg blue dress with lace trim around the collar. "And this one too." Before long I have six or seven dresses in my arms. Fortunately some of them are less fancy and seem suitable for working in a kitchen. She even gives me a couple of belts so I can cinch in the dresses to fit better until I have a chance to alter them.

"I'm sure this is more than enough," I tell her. "Thank you so much."

"Yes. I suppose we shouldn't overdo it." She reaches for what looks like an overnight bag. It's made of pastel tapestry, and judging by the designer name, I suspect it was expensive. "Let's pack them in this so you don't have to traipse across the grounds with an armload of dresses."

I thank her again.

"You're very welcome. Consider yourself part of our family, Rachel."

To my surprise my eyes are filling with tears. "Thank you. That means so much to me." And suddenly she's hugging me and I am telling her all about my parents' recent divorce, spilling my guts about how my mom is losing her house and moving to this cheesy condo. "And she's got this strange man helping her. For all I know he's planning to live there too."

"I'm so sorry." She gives me a handkerchief. "The world is so full of sin and heartache. Everyone seems so hopeless out there."

"I feel like I've lost my home and my family." I blot my wet cheeks. "Like I don't belong anywhere anymore."

"Well, you belong here, Rachel." She squeezes me. "We're your family now. And don't you forget it."

I thank her again. Then feeling self-conscious for opening up like this, I tell her I should probably get back to work.

"First you should take those dresses back to your cabin and hang them up," she commands. "Otherwise they will smell just like onions."

I grimace, holding up my hands. "I've been chopping onions."

She wrinkles her nose. "I noticed." Celeste goes over to a built-in dresser and removes a couple of bottles, handing them to me. One is perfume and the other is lotion. "Here, take these. And if Miriam gives you a bad time, just tell her I gave them to you."

"You're like my fairy godmother."

She laughs. "Just remember that God is the giver of every good and perfect gift."

I nod as we exit her closet. "I'll remember that."

As I carry the travel bag full of dresses back to my cabin, I feel unexpectedly happy. Celeste was so warm and generous and welcomed me like family. Maybe this really is going to become my home . . . permanently.

CHAPTER 13

I change into one of Celeste's dresses—a relatively plain one with a pleasant plaid in varying shades of blue, but still much nicer than Miriam's old castoff. Anyway, this dress seems suitable for kitchen work. Of course, I'd rather be wearing black-and-white checked cook's pants and a sleek white chef's jacket, but that wouldn't do around here. I remember to take my old Nadine's uniform with me, planning to give it to Josiah so he can drop it off with his delivery tomorrow.

I took time to write Nadine a short note earlier this morning. Not apologizing exactly since I did nothing wrong. But I attempted to express my sadness for how things ended. I also told her that I hope someday she'll find out the truth about what really happened. As I tuck the note into the shirt of the skimpy uniform, I can't believe how the Nadine era seems like another world to me now. I roll the uniform and note into a bundle and stick it under my arm. Hopefully no one will ask me about it.

"You're just in time to make the green salad," Eleanor tells me as I stash my rolled-up pink-and-white bundle on a shelf of dusty cookbooks. "The lettuce and carrots are in the fridge. I usually chop the lettuce and grate the carrots."

"That's all?"

She gives me a funny look, then shakes her head. When I go to the fridge, I'm dismayed to see only iceberg lettuce. "Do you mind if I use some other ingredients?" I call out.

"I don't care what you do," she says in a terse tone. "Just make sure there's enough for a hundred people."

"That's how many eat here?"

"Give or take."

I can tell she's in no mood to talk. Besides, judging by the clock, there isn't time. Spying a basket, I grab it and hurry out to the garden. There, with Hannah's help, I quickly gather a nice variety of vegetables—leafy greens, peppers, tomatoes, green onions, and all sorts of things I plan to mix with some of the iceberg lettuce.

"Now that's a salad I can get into." Hannah helps me carry fresh produce back to the kitchen. "I just hope Eleanor doesn't throw a fit."

"I know." I cringe to think of rubbing Eleanor wrong on my first day. "I'll try to keep things low-key."

"Good luck."

It's fun putting the salad together. I even get Lydia to help me wash produce and do some chopping. Next I toss all the ingredients in several big aluminum bowls. And finally I make my own dressing—a mixture of canola oil (although I'm wishing for olive) and apple cider vinegar (but I prefer balsamic), some dry mustard, garlic powder, salt, and a dollop of mayo just to bind it together. Okay, it's not the best dressing ever, but considering my choice of ingredients, it's not bad. Then just before lunch, I toss the salads and set them out on the buffet table, hoping for the best.

Today's menu consists of meatloaf, mashed potatoes, rolls, and my salad. And if I do say so, my salad is the best part of the meal. And it looks like others agree, because I hear positive comments being made to Eleanor about it. Clearly it's not a typical salad for them. And naturally they assume she made it. When it's time to clean up, I see that there's no leftover salad.

"Seems that your salad was appreciated," she tells me. "I guess you should be the official salad chef." She chuckles like this is a good joke.

"That's fine with me. I love making salads."

"Good, because I don't." She frowns. "But I expect more than just salads from you, Rachel. And I expect you to put more time into the kitchen than you did this morning."

"I realize that." I set some of the serving dishes near the sink where Bethany and Lydia are rinsing. "And that's not a problem for me."

After we get things cleaned up and a fair amount of prep work done for the evening meal, Eleanor announces that we get an hour break. "But I expect you back here at four o'clock sharp."

"No problem." I retrieve my rolled-up bundle of pink and white and thankfully no one seems to notice.

It feels good to be outside. And it's a beautiful day. To my delight I spy the delivery truck parked in its usual place outside of the dairy barn. But I don't see Josiah around. Even so, I open the passenger door and set my uniform on the seat. He'll know what to do with it. Then I think I'll wander around the dairy a bit, hoping to bump into Josiah. Instead I run into Miriam, just emerging from the dairy. Now I remember this is about the time she finishes her shift. I wave, acting like I'm not the least bit surprised to see her.

"Well, look at you," she says as she joins me. "Did you already sew yourself a dress?"

I smirk at her. "I'll admit I'm a good seamstress, but even I couldn't sew a dress this fast." Realizing my chances of catching Josiah have just been wiped out, I tell her I'm on my way home, pretending that I came this way to walk back to the cabin with her.

"So where did you get the dress?"

Searching the grounds for Josiah as we walk, I tell her a little about my visit with Celeste this morning. However, I'm careful not to say too much. I got what Celeste was hinting at—that visits to the reverend's home were special and something to be treated with respect. For all I know, Miriam has never even been inside. In fact, that's my assumption. Because I cannot imagine her approving of the elegant and expensive furnishings I saw today. It just doesn't mesh with her frugal values. In fact, I'm anxious to speak to Josiah about this. I'm curious as to what he thinks.

My eyes light up as we pass by the bench. But I look away quickly. I don't want Miriam to spy me looking at the pebble on top of a big stone next to the bench. We both go into the cabin, and while she lies down for a rest, I open my "real testament," which I now understand is what people call this book. I wait until I hear the even sound of her breathing, then tiptoe out, barely closing the door.

I go over to the bench where I sit down and lean over in a prayer position, just like I've seen others doing. It's actually the perfect way to reach down and slip my fingers beneath the rock, feeling around until I touch paper, which I pull out and slip into my sleeve. My heart is pounding with anticipation, but I continue my prayer stance and actually attempt to pray, but I'm too distracted by the paper in my sleeve.

Before I stand and leave, I remember to brush the pebble off the big stone—the sign that I've retrieved my message. I hurry back to the cabin, quietly go inside, and once I'm safely in the bathroom, I remove the note and read the simple message.

Meet me at the footbridge over the creek at 7:45.

I feel slightly dismayed that it's not more interesting than that. But I understand his need to be careful. Of course he's cautious. What if someone found the note? He doesn't want anyone to suspect he's setting up a secret meeting with me. Even so, I cannot wait. And I'm tempted to change into a prettier dress, but this might raise Miriam's suspicions. As it is, I'll have to come up with some kind of excuse. Perhaps I can say that I'm working late in the kitchen. I'm sure that will happen sometimes.

I'm so excited about my "date" with Josiah that my fingers work quickly as I grate a small mountain of cheese. Tonight Eleanor has macaroni and cheese, peas, salad, rolls, and berry cobbler on the menu. I already know that I'm on salad patrol but hope I can do something else too. "What are your favorite things to cook?" I ask Eleanor as I set the cheese by where she's working.

"Favorite things?" She looks at me like I just asked if she wears briefs or boxers.

"You know, some chefs prefer desserts. Some like baking bread. Some only want to do entrées."

Her brows draw together. "I suppose I like baking best of all."

I smile at her. "Your baking is always delicious." And that's mostly true. Her breads and rolls, while predictable, are usually pretty good.

"Thank you." She pours the cheese into the sauce she's making, slowly stirring. "Although I'm not terribly fond of making desserts."

"I love making desserts."

"Really?" She tilts her head to one side. "Do you think you can handle making the berry cobbler?"

I nod eagerly. "Sure. I've made cobbler before."

"For a hundred people?"

I laugh. "No, of course not. But how hard can it be?"

She shrugs. "I guess you'll find out. My recipe is over there by the oven. Have at it."

I'm not surprised to see her recipe lacks creativity. But not wanting to rock the boat, I stick to it for the most part. However, I add a few additional ingredients like cinnamon and an assortment of berries. And I substitute real butter instead of shortening. Who wants to eat shortening? Also, I decide to brown some oatmeal and add it to the crust to make it crunchier. As I cook, I imagine Josiah eating what I'm making, and it fills me with so much joy that I could almost burst.

"You sure seem happy," Bethany says as she rinses a mixing bowl.

I smile and sigh. "It just feels like I'm where I belong."

She gives me a blank and slightly confused look. But then she smiles too. However, it's a forced smile.

Dinner gets even more compliments than lunch. Again they are directed to Eleanor and, like before, she brushes them off. And this time she doesn't make any comments to me. This gets me a little worried.

"I hope that I'm lightening your load," I tell her as we're all cleaning up. "I know how hard you've worked."

"Oh, well, hard work never hurt anyone."

After that we work quietly. And I'm hugely relieved when we're finished and it's 7:40 — just enough time to make it to the footbridge. However, I need to be careful about this.

"It's such a lovely evening," I say as I hang up my apron.

"I think I'll get some fresh air." Fortunately no one comments on this or offers to accompany me. And just like that, I'm out the door and on my way, just strolling along.

My heart is racing when I finally make it to the footbridge. But to my dismay I don't see Josiah. Even so I go onto the bridge, and when I'm halfway across I hear a whistle coming from the other side. I peer over and spot him waving from the shadows of the trees. Then acting nonchalant, I stroll on over and join him in the shadows.

"Come on," he whispers and, holding my hand, leads me through the woods down an overgrown trail until we finally emerge in a clearing. "Care to sit?" He waves his hand toward a fallen log.

"Don't mind if I do." I giggle as we sit down.

"I've missed you so much," he says as he slips his arms around me.

"Me too," I murmur. And now we are kissing and I feel like I'm floating . . . like I never want this moment to end. I never want him to be more than a few inches from me.

But then he stops kissing me and, placing both of his hands on my cheeks, looks deeply into my eyes. "We need to talk."

I try not to feel alarmed — but those are the four dreaded words. "About what?" I ask nervously.

"About us."

"*Us?*"

He smiles in a reassuring way. "It's going to be tricky to keep meeting, Rachel. Even today when I slipped that message beneath the rock, I got the feeling I was being watched."

"I know what you mean."

"We just have to be really careful."

I nod. "I know." Now I frown. "But I'm not totally sure why. I mean, I get that your uncle doesn't want — well, you know."

I can't bring myself to say that word—*fornication*. It just sounds so dirty. "But I don't see why we can't spend time together."

"Not like this," he tells me.

"Yes . . . I know."

"And after I left your note, I realize we need a code. I purposely didn't put our names on it, but I shouldn't have said meet me at the footbridge. If someone else found it, well, they'd have figured me out."

"That's true."

So he pulls out a small pad of paper, and we devise a code for meeting places as well as times. We both write down the code, then kiss again.

"As much as I'd like to sit here all night, we better get back. Otherwise, we'll both have some explaining to do."

Now I remember putting my uniform in his truck and quickly explain. "Do you mind leaving it at Nadine's for me?"

"Not at all." He stands, pulling me to my feet and giving me one last hug. "You go first. After crossing the bridge, you take the trail directly back to the cabins. I'll wind my way up the creek a bit before I cross back."

"When will we do this again?" I ask hopefully.

"Tomorrow night is study groups. But maybe we can meet for a few minutes before."

"Yes," I say eagerly.

"How about the garden at two thirty?" He gives me a sly look.

"Ah . . . the garden, which is really out behind the dairy barn, and two thirty plus five equals seven thirty."

"You got it."

"I feel like we're starring in a James Bond movie." I look down at my dress, then laugh. "Well, a very conservative James Bond movie."

He laughs too, kissing me one final time.

Then I take off with feet that feel light. And I can't help but imagine I'm on a great adventure as I make my way through the dusky woods and back across the bridge to my cabin, where Miriam is waiting for me with a suspicious expression.

"Why are you so late? I was about to go out looking for you."

"Oh, there was so much to do in the kitchen tonight." I kick off my shoes. "What a day. I had no idea there was so much work. But then I never cooked for a hundred people before." I continue to ramble on and on, and Miriam soon grows tired of my chatter.

"Please." She holds up her hands. "I like peace and quiet before bedtime." Then she changes into her long white night-gown and, just like last night, drops to her knees in front of her bed. Bowing her head, she remains there while I go into the bathroom and get ready for bed.

When I emerge from the bathroom, Miriam is standing in front of the narrow closet with the door open, staring at the colorful dresses I've hung in there. "Did Celeste give you all of these?" she asks in a suspicious tone.

"Yes. I thought it seemed overly generous, but she insisted."

Now Miriam turns to peer at me with narrowed eyes. "Why would she give you so many dresses?"

I bite my lip, trying to think of a good reason. I just shrug. "Maybe she felt sorry for me."

"Sorry? For you?"

So I tell her about my parents' divorce and my mom losing our home. I try to make it sound pathetic, hoping to distract her and eliminate her suspicions.

However, she seems completely unimpressed. "Well, if you want to exchange sad tales, perhaps I should share mine."

I sit on my bed and cross one leg over the other. "Sure, I'd love to hear your story."

But I am as unprepared for what she tells me as I am for the way she tells it. In a flat, unemotional monotone, she tells me how both her parents were killed in a car wreck that resulted from a flash flood when she was young. "After that I was sent to live with my mother's sister and her alcoholic husband. There I was sexually abused by my uncle and my cousins until I was fourteen and finally got the nerve to run away."

"Oh!" My hand is pressed over my mouth in horror. "I'm so sorry."

She shrugs. "Don't be. God has rescued me from that life of depravity." She peels back the covers on her bed and fluffs her pillow. "But next time you want to win my favor with a sob story, you might want to think again."

I want to say something more to her . . . something to make her feel better . . . to show her that I feel for her and am truly sorry for her pain. But I can think of nothing that sounds quite right. So I simply say good night.

been written specifically for women. Judging by the table of contents, it's about things like modesty, servitude, being a good wife, and preparing for motherhood. However, if I didn't know better, I'd think it had been written a couple of centuries ago. I want to question some of the things I'm hearing, but that wouldn't go over too well.

Besides that, I know I should be honored to be included. It's an elite group; I can just feel it. And although I'm clearly at the bottom of this feeding chain, I'm surprised I've been included at all. But at the same time, I'm flattered. And I'm slightly amazed at how I'm able to make myself fit in with these women. In some ways I probably fit in better with them than I do with people on the outside.

· · · · · · · · · ·

The next week passes with the reassuring regularity of an expected routine. No surprises. And although the work is demanding and tiring and it feels like Eleanor is putting more and more responsibility on me, I like the challenge. And I like that people seem to appreciate a varied menu with tasty food. That makes me feel good. And it feels good to fall into bed exhausted every night, knowing I've done my best and someone is noticing. Plus it's so quiet here that I sleep like a log.

Besides working in the kitchen, I participate in Miriam's advanced sewing class, and the women in there are impressed by my skills. I also attend all the church services as well as my women's study group. By the end of my second week here, I feel like I'm very much a part of this community. And I feel happy.

At the same time, I'm struggling with some guilt issues. I feel slightly hypocritical for my secret meetings with Josiah. I'm pretty sure that Celeste and Reverend Jim would not approve. And yet in a way I feel like they might secretly approve.

Celeste drops little hints, as if she's already planning a wedding for Josiah and me. And although it seems silly to consider marriage at my age, the idea is starting to grow on me. I don't mind that these women might be grooming me to become Josiah's wife. I think I would make a good wife, and I can imagine spending the rest of my life with Josiah.

But when I imagine what my mom or some of my friends would say, I realize I could be living in a dream world. And that's when I start to feel very confused. For that reason I've decided not to think about what people on the outside might say or do. Like Reverend Jim says·again and again, "The world despises us because they despise God. We should expect nothing less than hatred and persecution from them."

That's just one more reason to be thankful that I don't have access to my cell phone. I can't imagine having conversations with anyone on the outside. Even when I speak to Mom, I keep it brief and guarded.

"You're mature for your age," Celeste tells me after my third study group meeting. "Some people grow up faster than others. I can tell you're one of those."

"Thanks," I murmur, trying to imitate the humility I've seen demonstrated by the other women in this group. They seem to be that way naturally, but I'm determined I can be more like that. I want to be more like that. I realize pride and arrogance are of the devil.

"But I'm sure I have a long ways to go," I tell her as I walk her to her house. For some reason accompanying her home has become a habit. A habit I enjoy. It makes me feel special being with Celeste. I've almost reconciled myself to the jealous glances this earns me. Because I'm beginning to realize this is their problem not mine.

"Yes, we all have a long way to go, Rachel, but you're coming along very nicely."

The way Celeste says this reminds me of something Eleanor might say while checking on a large roast. However, I know Celeste means this as a compliment. And coming from the wife of our leader, it is high praise indeed. I'm working so hard to fit into my new family. Sometimes I question myself and my motives on this—am I trying too hard? Am I trying to fit in, or am I simply trying to outshine the others? If it's the latter, I need to work harder on humbling myself.

"The devil uses pride to devour the soul," Reverend Jim says often. "Servitude and humility are the antidote to pride."

Now I follow Miriam's example every night, by hitting my knees before going to bed. At first I just did this because I knew it would please her. It was also a good way to deflect her inquisitions regarding my whereabouts after spending time with Josiah. But after a while, I began to sincerely apply myself to my prayers.

Reverend Jim says that God expects us to pray regularly. He says that each minute we spend in God's presence secures three minutes in heaven—whether it's time spent in meetings or servitude or prayer, it all adds up. And since eternity is so much longer than our earthly lives, we need to ensure that we have plenty of time stockpiled for later use.

But when I mention things like this to Josiah, thinking he'll be proud of me for my spiritual devotion, he seems slightly indifferent. Sometimes he even changes the subject. And sometimes I wonder if we're in different places spiritually. *What if I outgrow him?* The idea of this is so disturbing that I can barely consider it. Because the truth is: Josiah is the reason I'm here.

Without Josiah I wouldn't have done any of this. But that's even more disturbing. God is supposed to be the reason I'm here.

By mid-August, I notice that there can be a little nip in the air in the evenings. That's because we're in the mountains. According to Celeste, there's still plenty of warm weather left. But because of the cooling temperatures, Josiah decided to build a protective structure in the woods for us—our secret hideaway. He's worked hard to pile up old logs and branches, creating a small hut that's so well camouflaged, you can't even see it until you nearly stumble onto it. Down a twisting path and a good distance from the footbridge, our private getaway reminds me of a hobbit house.

Josiah says we'll really appreciate our little hut when the weather starts to change. "I heard it gets quite cold here when summer ends," he told me the first time I saw his building project. Of course, that was a startling thought to me. Not that it will get cold. But that summer will end. Because that's something I've tried to block out. When summer ends my mom will expect me to come home. And resume my life and finish high school.

I've only talked to Mom three times since moving here. And our conversations get briefer each time. I almost get the feeling she's as relieved as I am when I tell her I have to go. Like she's so caught up in her own bachelorette lifestyle, she doesn't really care about me anymore. For all I know, she might even be worried that I'll be an intrusion in her compact condo.

Yet at the same time, I'm not sure how she'd react if I told her I was never coming home. She could easily play the parent card and insist I return. But then I can simply point out that I turn eighteen in late September. I'll be considered an adult then. How can she tell me what to do?

"You're changing," Josiah tells me, interrupting my stewing over what feels like my very uncertain future. We're both reclining on a mattress of evergreen needles, and everything smells so fresh and green in here that after a day spent toiling in the kitchen, it's a tonic for my soul.

"What do you mean I'm changing?"

He rolls over on his side and, pushing a strand of hair off my forehead, studies me. "I'm not sure how exactly. But you seem different."

"Different good or different bad?"

He shrugs. "I'm not sure. Just different."

I sit up now, looking intently at him. "I'm really trying to fit in here. I'm working hard in the kitchen. Attending my groups. Are you saying I'm not doing it right? I'm not trying hard enough?"

Now he looks perplexed. "Maybe that's it. Maybe you're trying *too hard*, Rachel. Maybe you're losing yourself by trying so hard to be like . . ." He sighs, then looks up at the thatched roof overhead.

"Like what?"

He looks at me with a creased forehead. "Like the rest of them."

I frown at him. "What's wrong with that? Isn't that why we're here? To change and get better?"

"What if changing isn't better?"

"What if it is?"

Closing his eyes, he exhales loudly.

"What's wrong?" I ask. Suddenly I feel worried. Are we drifting apart? I don't think I could do this without him.

He reaches up and grabs me by the shoulders, pulling me down on him and then we are kissing. And, as usual, when we're kissing, I forget about everything else. But when the kissing's over, I feel guilty. *As usual.* I feel guilty and confused.

Then we take our different routes back to our cabins, and I hurry to get ready for bed. Avoiding Miriam's piercing eyes, I fall down on my knees and silently beg God to forgive me.

The next day I'm surprised to cross paths with Monique. Oh, I suppose it's possible we've crossed paths before, but I didn't recognize her. And seeing her now, dressed in what looks like one of Miriam's castoff dresses and with her harsh makeup removed and her hair pulled back in a single braid, she looks completely different. Even her tattoos are hidden. Although I suspect they're still there, simply concealed by the long sleeves and skirt.

"Rachel," she hisses at me as I'm heading for the restroom in the dining hall. It's a few minutes before dinner, and I'm trying to grab a quick break before the place starts filling up.

I blink at her. "Monique?"

"Yes, of course. Who did you think it was?"

"Sorry." I make an uneasy smile and nod to the door. "I have to use the facilities."

"Good. I'll talk to you in there."

Once we're inside the ladies' room, Monique looks around, to confirm that we're alone, and then scoots the tall stainless-steel wastebasket in front of the door.

"What are you doing?"

"For security." She nods to a stall. "Go ahead and do your thing. Just listen. Okay?"

Not seeing how I can argue, since I really need to go, I enter the stall and proceed to "do my thing." While I go, she is rambling, complaining, and whining.

"I've got to get out of here," she says as I flush the toilet. "I've had it with this place. Everyone here is nuts and it's getting nuttier every day."

I don't know what to say, but I'm glad she put the trash container by the door because I really wouldn't want anyone else to hear her going on like this. I come out, glancing curiously at her as I meticulously wash my hands.

"Deacon Clarence is insisting that I marry him," she tells me in a hushed tone.

"*What?*" I turn to stare at her as I dry my hands. She's clearly crazy.

"You *heard* me, Rachel. Deacon Clarence plans to take me as his wife — I mean, like any day now."

"But he's married," I say as I toss the towel in the wastebasket still blocking the door. "I even know his wife."

Monique rolls her eyes. "Are you serious?"

"Yes. He's definitely married. His wife's name is Cindy and he has three kids and — "

"No, I mean are you seriously *that* clueless?"

"What do you mean?" I tip my head to one side, trying to figure her out.

"I mean are you really that naive, Rachel? You don't know that these dudes believe it's just fine to have multiple wives? I thought you were all cozy with Celeste and Jim. Haven't they mentioned this to you by now?"

"No." I firmly shake my head. "And I don't believe you."

She uses a foul word. "And I thought you could help me."

"Help you . . . how?" I edge nervously toward the door, hoping to move that can and make a fast break out of here before she totally flips out on me. Monique clearly sounds like she's losing it — big time.

"Help me get out of here, Rachel. I want you to talk to Josiah for me. I know you guys are close. And I know he makes deliveries. But I never get a chance to speak to him. Just tell him I need to leave and ask if I can ride with him when he's—"

Just then the door moves, bumping noisily into the can. I hurry over and slide it out of the way, smiling innocently as Bethany comes in.

"What's wrong with the door?" she asks.

"Nothing," I assure her. Then without looking back at Monique, I hurry out of there. I don't know why she's blocking doors and spouting such crazy stuff, but the girl needs some serious help. Just not from me. And not from Josiah. Monique is trouble. And someone higher up needs to deal with her.

Fortunately this is one of our rendezvous evenings, and I can't wait to sneak out into the woods and tell Josiah what I just heard. Maybe we can both laugh about it. And maybe Josiah can talk to his uncle, suggest that Monique take a few days off. I've heard from Miriam that working in the dairy is one of the toughest jobs here. Maybe Monique just needs a break. Or some counseling.

But when I finally make it to our secret hideaway and spill my story to Josiah, he becomes very quiet. Too quiet.

"Is she losing her mind?" I press. "I mean, first she barricades me with her in the bathroom. Then she announces that Deacon Clarence is going to marry her. And then she tells me that she wants you to help her get out of here. I mean . . . *seriously?*"

"Rachel . . ." He sits up and, wrapping his arms around his knees, watches me closely, and I can see him weighing his response in his mind.

This worries me. "*What?* What is going on? Do you know?"

"Do you really *not* know?"

"Not know *what?*" Suddenly my chest tightens and my heart races, and not in a good way. It's more like how you feel after waking from a nightmare or if you need to run for your life.

"Hasn't Celeste told you . . . told you . . . about . . . ?"

"Told me about what?"

He gets a grim expression now. "Hasn't she informed you that deacons in the church are allowed to marry more than one wife?"

"What the — ?" I sit up straight, glaring at him. "You cannot be serious. Are you telling me that Monique was telling me the truth?"

He just nods.

"Well, that's just unbelievable."

"Surely you've heard about religious groups like this before. Churches that have spun off of other churches."

"Is that what this is — a spin-off of GEF?"

He looks tired. "I tried to make myself believe it wasn't. But I think I was wrong."

I feel blindsided. How did I miss this? Did I see signs and was simply in deep denial? My head feels like it's spinning. "I'm so confused."

"I'm sorry, Rachel. I thought you knew. Surely you've heard of these kinds of groups before. It's not terribly uncommon in the States."

I frown at him. "Well, sure, I watched *Sister Wives* a couple of times back when it first came out. But it was like watching a freak show. And to be honest, it was pretty hard to believe. I honestly thought they made the whole thing up for ratings — and the people were just actors."

"Some people believe it's perfectly acceptable to live like that. Some say it's biblical. Don't forget that some of the fathers of our faith had multiple wives. Including Abraham, Jacob, David, Solomon . . . I could go on. My uncle has shown me these passages in the Bible enough times. And I mean the *real* Bible too. Not just my uncle's real testament."

I peer curiously at him. "Do you believe that? I mean, that it's okay to have multiple wives?"

"No, I don't think so. Not personally. But at the same time I try not to judge others. I try to be open. Still, it's a fine balance sometimes." He pushes his hair back with a frustrated look. "I'm still trying to figure these things out."

"And I'm still trying to wrap my head around this. You're not pulling my leg, are you, Josiah? Just for clarity, are you actually saying that Reverend Jim and the deacons honestly believe it's okay to commit bigamy?"

"Some have more than just two wives." He shakes his head sadly. "So you really didn't know . . . I just assumed it would've been discussed in Celeste's group."

Now I try to remember. "There's been a lot of teaching about being a wife and a mother, but I never heard it put quite like that—I've never heard anyone mention multiple wives."

"Maybe they're trying to break you in slowly."

"Break me in?"

"Well, you're here, Rachel. What did you expect? And my aunt likes you a lot. I'm sure they're trying to indoctrinate you."

"Indoctrinate me?" I find this term offensive. It smacks of brainwashing.

"Whatever you call it. They're grooming you. Surely, you can see that."

"What about you?" I demand.

"What about me?"

"Well, you're here too. Are they indoctrinating you as well?"

"I'm sure they're trying. Uncle Jim meets with me regularly. Like I said, he keeps telling me about our fathers of faith and their multiple wives. But he knows I'm resistant to some things."

"Like polygamy?"

He takes in a deep breath, then just chuckles. "You actually sound jealous." His tone has a slight teasing sound to it. And that irritates me.

"Of course I'd be jealous if I thought you were like that." I stand up. "Because if you think I'd settle for being married to someone who wants more than one wife, you better think again." Okay, even as I say this, I can hear how ridiculous I sound. It's not as if he's asking me to marry him. I move for the door. "I need to get back to my cabin."

"Don't leave like this."

"Like what?" I brush loose pine needles from my dress.

"Angry. Don't go away angry, Rachel."

"I'm sorry," I say in a hurt tone. "But this is too much to absorb. I think I'm in shock."

"Then stay. Let's talk it through."

"Talk it through?" I'm blinking back tears now. It feels like my world is crumbling. Like no one is what I thought. Even Josiah no longer seems to be who I'd imagined him to be.

"Rachel," he pleads. "Wait."

"No wonder Monique wants to leave." I duck down to slip out of the opening to the hut. And I take off running through the woods. As I run, I hope he'll chase after me. I hope he'll grab me and hold me in his arms and reassure me that everything is okay, that he'll tell me it was all just a bad joke. And that no one has multiple wives here.

But as I run, I realize he's not coming after me. I turn to look behind me as I approach the creek. But he's not there. And finally, as I hurry across the footbridge again, it's only the sound of the creek and my own lonely footsteps that I hear.

CHAPTER 15

"**W**hat is wrong with you?" Miriam demands when I burst into the cabin. "And where have you been?"

I look directly at her, gauging what and how much I want to say.

"Tell me," she insists. "Or I shall go to Reverend Jim."

I collapse on my bed and just cry. I feel so lost. So confused. So betrayed. My head hurts from trying to understand all this.

"What is it, child?" she gently asks me, sitting on the edge of my bed and stroking my hair. "What has happened to you?"

I sit up and look at her with tears streaming down my face. "I just found out—I just heard—that—that the deacons have multiple wives here." I stare at her, trying to discern her reaction. "Is that true?"

She stands, turning her back to me.

"Is it true?"

She is pacing now, the hem of her long nightgown swishes back and forth across the braided rug as she paces. Her arms are folded tightly across her front and her expression is grim.

"Tell me," I demand. "Josiah says it's true. Monique says it's true. Is it true?"

"Of course, it's true. You little fool!" She turns, facing me with angry gray eyes. "Do you honestly expect me to believe you didn't know that already?"

"I didn't! I swear I didn't."

She shrugs. "Well, now you do."

"But *why*?" I go over to her, glaring at her with clenched fists. "Why is this okay? And what about you, Miriam? None of the deacons seems intent on forcing you to marry. I don't see you ever becoming a *sister wife*."

She reaches her hand up and—just like that—slaps me right across the face. I'm so stunned I don't know what to say. I slowly back away from her, holding a hand to my stinging cheek in horror.

Now Miriam begins to sob quietly. "I'm sorry, Rachel," she finally says in a trembling voice. "I had no right to do that."

I feel guilty for provoking her. "I'm sorry too. I shouldn't have said what I did . . . about you."

She sits on her bed, holding her head in her hands, still crying. "You are right. I will never become a wife, nor will I become a sister wife. Never."

I go over and sit in the chair by her bed. My head feels like it's going to explode. So much is going through it—crazy thoughts, confused thoughts—flying about and bouncing up and down and left and right. I can't begin to grasp them. I will never understand.

"I'm so confused," I admit. "I thought this place was about getting to know God, about serving him, about being pure and good and holy. And I was trying."

She looks at me with defiant eyes. "It is! It's about all those things."

I study her closely, seeing the sincere determination in her eyes. "You know, Miriam, I believe it is. At least for you."

"Not only for me. We *all* want those things. But it takes time and work. We're not perfect . . . but we are working toward perfection — together. We're learning and growing, and if we obey our leadership and humble ourselves, we will get there — together."

I let out a long, tired sigh.

"I can see your faith is shaken." She removes a tattered handkerchief from her nightgown sleeve and loudly blows her nose.

I nod. "That's for sure."

"But it's only because you don't understand. You see in the glass dimly, but someday you'll see face-to-face."

"I don't see how."

"I was like that . . . once." She begins to tell me about what happened after she ran away from her abusive uncle and cousins. "The Davis family took me in. I mean, Reverend Jim's parents. Oh, he wasn't a reverend then, but he was a very special person. I could see it. And everyone who met him knew Jim was brilliant and gifted . . . and special. His parents ran a cattle station outside of Melbourne and they took me in as if I was their own. Jim had just returned from his mission and was managing the business for them. But he began to question his parents' church — God's Eternal Family. Despite his doubts regarding their doctrine, he remained active in the church."

She sniffed. "And he tried to make the elders understand his thoughts, but they rebuked him and eventually exiled him from fellowship. But by then he had many devoted followers who respected his insight and teaching." She sighs. "He was truly inspired. He could even predict the future."

"How so?" I demand.

She lists a number of events. Everything from politics and the environment to the global economy. "When everyone else

was losing money, the people following Jim's teaching were prof-
iting. God was blessing them above and beyond what they could
imagine." She waves her hand. "That's how he was able to
purchase this place—for cash. How he was able to develop it
and do all that he does. God blesses Reverend Jim unlike anyone
else." She looks intently at me now. "It's because Reverend Jim is
God's chosen prophet."

I sigh. "I know, I've heard all that before. And I was starting
to believe it. But now I'm confused. I just don't understand this
thing about multiple wives."

"Do you not understand we are living in the last days? Have
you not listened to the reverend's sermons? Can you not see the
signs of the times?"

"Yes, I know about all that. And it makes sense." Okay, it
doesn't always make sense, but I try to believe the reverend's
teaching. I wanted to believe it.

"Not only Reverend Jim, but other prophets have predicted
that in the last days, one man will have many wives. It's in the
Bible as well as the real testament. It's simply what must be. To
question this is to question all of the teaching that surrounds the
last days."

"But I don't understand," I tell her. "I don't want to question, but I don't understand why one man would need more
than one wife. Why isn't one wife enough?"

"It's because the world is so full of evil." Her eyes grow wide.
"Sin abounds everywhere. You've heard the reverend preach on
this. Men in the world are especially vulnerable to sinful desire.
They are easily tempted by the evil lust of their flesh. Your own
father allowed his sinful lust to destroy your family. Now your
mother is alone, right?"

I barely nod, trying to get this.

"Because of the sinful lusts of men, there are not enough good men to go around. For that reason one good man must take in numerous wives — to love and protect them and to create a happy family unit and to raise righteous offspring. Surely you can understand that."

"If you really believe that, why don't you become a sister wife?" I ask, trying to put it more gently. "I mean, don't you want to be part of a family like that too?"

She sits up straighter. "I told Reverend Jim long ago that because of my past, I prefer not to marry. He understands and respects that. He says that remaining single is an exceptional gift. A gift I've been blessed with."

"And you're happy?"

She nods firmly, and then we both just sit there in silence. Finally she points to the alarm clock by her bed. "But it's very late and my shift begins early. Unless you have some very important questions, I must go to sleep."

. . . .

After a very sleepless night, I get up and shower and dress. Then, still feeling thoroughly confused and fairly dismayed, I leave for work. My feet feel heavy today, and I'm trying to decide what to do. In the darkness of night, I felt a desperate need to escape this place, but with the sun shining brightly in the clear blue sky and seeing all the natural beauty around me, it no longer looks so cut and dried. As I walk down the path from the cabin, I realize it's not that easy to sort everything out.

I'm just going past the bench when I notice a pebble on the big stone — Josiah's sign that he's left a message for me. Surprised, I pause to sit on the edge of the bench and bend my head as if to pray. Then I slip my hand down and extract the rolled-up note.

Meet me. 2:30.

I tuck the note into the pocket of my dress and continue on to the dining hall, but before I get there, I'm surprised to be met by Reverend Jim. He greets me with a sunny smile.

"You're just the girl I was looking for."

Suddenly I wonder if I've done something wrong. "I was just on my way to work. I hope I'm not late."

"No worries," he says. "I was just speaking to Eleanor." He chuckles. "I'm afraid she's not very happy with what I told her."

"Oh?"

"She tried to hide her disappointment, but I told her that your cooking skills are needed in another capacity."

"Another capacity?"

He grins. "Celeste came up with a wonderful idea. From now on, you are going to come and cook for us."

I'm sure my shock registers on my face.

"Eleanor will forgive me," he says. "And I promised to send her a couple more kitchen helpers to make up for losing you. But your culinary gift will be better utilized in our home. Do you have a problem with that?"

"No-no," I stammer, "of course not."

He pats me on the back. "Fantastic. You can report to Celeste straightaway. She's waiting for you."

As I thank him, I feel numb. But as I turn and walk toward his house, I feel trapped. However, when Celeste greets me, she is so warm and kind that I question my feelings. Maybe I'm wrong about them.

"We are absolutely thrilled to have you join us," she tells me. "I don't know if Jim told you about my cooking skills, but let's just say it's not my best talent." She giggles. "Having you take this over is absolutely thrilling." She leads me through a swinging door into a spacious, attractive kitchen. "I hope you'll feel right at home here."

"It's beautiful." I run my hand over a granite countertop, taking in the large stainless-steel appliances, including an eight-burner commercial gas stove. "It's a dream kitchen."

Now Kellie comes in to join us, and I wonder if she will resent me. I know she works here, and I had assumed she was the cook. "We're overjoyed to have her, aren't we, Kellie?"

Kellie nods. "Neither Celeste nor I are very good cooks."

"But Kellie will assist you," Celeste promises. Now she turns to Kellie. "And will you show Rachel her room?"

"Of course." Kellie waves to the door on the opposite end of the kitchen. "We're in the north wing."

"I didn't realize there were wings," I say as she leads me down a hallway.

"It's not as lovely as the south wing. But that's because Celeste is the first wife."

"First wife?" I try not to sound alarmed.

Kellie turns to look at me. "Surely, you know Celeste is the first wife."

"Well, yes, of course. Are you the second wife?"

Kellie laughs as she leads me up a narrow staircase. "I wish."

"Oh . . ." I take in a quick breath. "I'm sorry. To be honest, I'm not sure how many wives the reverend has. Or, uh, how many people I'll be cooking for."

Kellie pauses at the landing on top. "Celeste has three children. Jan has four with another on the way."

I'm stunned. "Seven children live in this house? I mean, I've seen a couple, but I had no idea there were seven. It's so quiet."

"The children's wing is on the other side of the house. And they have their own small kitchen in there. That's Jan's territory. The kids have breakfast and lunch in her wing."

"I don't think I've met Jan."

"She doesn't get out much. She's in charge of all the kids. I help her sometimes, especially with her pregnancy. It's kind of wearing her out. She's over forty and you know what they say about that."

"Oh, yeah." I act like I know.

"I'll have kids someday, but I've only been here a few months, so there's no hurry. Anyway, you asked how many. That's a total of eleven to cook for. Well, twelve now that you're here. It's a good thing the dining room seats twelve."

"You mean I'll be eating with, uh, the family? I thought I was just working as the cook."

Kellie frowns. "Well, you're the cook. But you're joining the family, right?"

I force a smile. "I guess so. It was kind of a surprise."

"Well, that's just how Reverend Jim works. He keeps us on our toes." She opens the door and flicks on the lights to reveal a pale blue bedroom. With a queen bed, a pair of bedside tables and lamps, a dark blue easy chair, and a long matching dresser, it reminds me of a hotel room.

"I didn't realize I was going to be living here. Do you think they'd mind if I remained at the cabin? With Miriam?"

Kellie laughs. "You're kidding, right?"

I give her a blank look.

"You'd rather live there than here?" She waves her hand. "This is a really nice room, Rachel. Much better than living with Miriam. I should know. I was with her for a full year before coming here. You sure don't hear me complaining."

I bite into my lip, gauging my words. "Can I ask you something?"

"Sure. What?"

"Well, living here like this . . . well, does it mean I'm expected to be a, uh, a sister wife too?"

Kellie throws back her head and laughs loudly. "Are you serious?"

I shrug, feeling foolish.

"No, silly. You're just the cook." Now she frowns at me. "Don't tell me you're hoping for something more."

"No, not at all. I just, uh, wondered."

"Well, Jim — I mean the reverend — he told me that three is the perfect number." She holds up three fingers.

"Three?"

"Wives."

"Oh . . ." I nod in relief.

"Besides, he's so busy running this dairy and preaching and everything. I honestly don't think he has time for any more wives."

"How would you feel if he did?" Even as the words are out, I wish I could grab them back.

Kellie scowls. "Well, I really don't think I need to worry about that. As the reverend says, we shouldn't worry about tomorrow. Today has enough trouble to keep us occupied."

I nod. "Yes, you're right."

"Anyway," she narrows her eyes at me, "I don't see why you're concerned about that. I thought you were Josiah's girl."

"Yes," I say eagerly. "I mean, I hope so. Josiah and I really do care about each other. I mean, we're good friends."

"You're lucky. Josiah seems like a good guy. And the reverend thinks of him as a son."

I nod again. "Yes. You're right, Josiah's a good guy. A really good guy." Now I feel bad for the way I ran out on him yesterday. I'm so relieved he wants to meet with me tonight. Maybe when I tell him about this—about being moved into his uncle's house—maybe he can help me figure things out. Because suddenly, it seems clear. Crystal clear. I can't stay here. It's not what I thought it was . . . it's not how I want to live my life. I want out.

"Celeste told me to go with you to collect your things." Kellie turns off the lights. "She wants you all moved in here with plenty of time to fix lunch, because the deacons' wives are coming today." I can tell by the way she says this, it's no small thing.

"Oh?" I follow her back down the stairs. "How many guests will there be?" I realize there are six deacons, but I have no idea how many wives that makes.

"Twenty-three counting Celeste and me. Jan will be with the children."

I quickly do the math. "That's more than three wives per deacon."

She laughs again. "Well, three might be Reverend Jim's special number, but he rewards his deacons differently. Now we better hurry if we want to have lunch ready by one."

As we walk across the grounds to the cabins, Kellie rambles on about which wives belong to which deacon. I'm surprised she can keep them all straight. "I'm kind of like Celeste's assistant," she explains when we reach my cabin. "She expects me to handle a lot of stuff. But I don't mind."

She goes in with me, watching as I remove the dresses from the closet as well as my own personal things, cramming them all into the bag. Before I leave, I suddenly remember my paycheck from Nadine's. I had slipped it under the mattress. But I don't want to leave it behind.

"Ready?" she asks.

I go over to my old bed, pretending to straighten it. "I wonder if I should leave Miriam a note." I slip my hand underneath the thin mattress, feeling around.

"Oh, don't worry about her. She's used to losing roommates."

Finally I locate the envelope holding my check, but as I remove it, I realize that Kellie is watching me closely.

"What's that?"

I hold it up with a sheepish smile, explaining that it was my final check from the place I worked before coming here.

"But why were you hiding it?"

"I, uh, wasn't really hiding it," I say. "Just keeping it safe."

She reaches out for it. "I'll see that it gets to a safe place."

"But I—"

"Look, Rachel, if you haven't figured this out already, it's time you did." She gives me a stern look. "Reverend Jim is the authority here. No one questions him. And any money or anything of value goes into his safe." She puts her open palm closer to me. "Unless you'd like to take this conversation up with him?"

I hand over my check and she smiles. "Really, it'll be in a safer place now anyway."

As we walk back to the reverend's house, I wonder if Josiah knows about his uncle's safe or how to get into it. I wonder if he can help me to get my stuff out of the storage shed too. And maybe I don't even care about those things or the check. More than ever, I want out of here. I know it's time to leave this place. The sooner the better. Maybe Josiah can take both me and Monique out of here first thing tomorrow. Even if we have to sit in the back of the truck with the ice cream, it will be worth it.

···[CHAPTER 16]················

My morning is spent in the kitchen, scrambling to get everything ready for the wives' luncheon. And while I appreciate the distraction of cooking, as soon as lunch is served—thankfully by several of the teenage girls—I am allowed a short break. At first I imagine I'll be able to slip out, but then I realize, thanks to the buffet-style lunch, the wives are sitting in the large main room and I can't make it to the front entrance without being spotted.

A little more snooping around and I discover that the other doors, which all lead out to the pretty landscaped backyard, also offer no escape because the grounds back there are bordered by a tall rock wall and a sturdy iron gate. Short of scaling the wall, there's no way out. This place is very secure, complete with what appears to be a state-of-the-art security system. Was it created this way to keep people out . . . or to keep people in?

As I sit in my room, looking down on the backyard—which is looking more and more like a prison yard—I realize I might also have a challenge meeting Josiah tonight. Somehow I've got to get word to him. So I begin to concoct a plan. After the luncheon ends and the women all leave, I approach Celeste. "I hope you liked the lunch," I say to her and naturally she responds positively.

"Thanks," I tell her. "As I was cooking, I remembered that the garden has some lovely tomatoes right now. And the raspberries are really coming in good. And the corn looked just about ready to pick the other day." I sigh. "It was a shame I didn't think to bring some of those things up to the house."

Celeste's eyes light up. "Corn on the cob?"

"Yes," I say, hoping the corn's really ready. "Both white and yellow. And, of course, there's not enough of it to feed everyone. Hannah said it was kind of experimental. But I'm sure it's tasty."

"I'll send Kellie over there to—"

"I don't know if Kellie really understands how to select good produce," I tell her. "If you want the best, I should go and get it myself. That's what all good chefs do."

"You're right." She nods. "Go ahead."

I look at the clock above the fireplace. Josiah should be home from making deliveries by now. "I can make it back in plenty of time to have dinner ready," I assure her. "Kellie said you eat at six thirty."

"That's right." She looks uneasy now. "Should I send Kellie with you? To help carry things?"

"No. I'd rather Kellie stay here to do some prep work in the kitchen." I hold up a piece of paper. "I've listed some things for her to do. I really want tonight's dinner to be special."

Celeste beams at me. "I'm so glad you've come to us, Rachel. I can just tell that life's going to be much better with you here."

With a large basket over my arm, I hurry from the big house. Walking quickly across the grounds, I try to understand how Celeste can live like she does. How is she willing to share her husband with two other wives? But even as I ponder this, I think I'm starting to get it. A favorite saying around here is "many hands make light work." For Celeste to have Kellie helping her to manage the home and Jan supervising the children and now with me doing the cooking, her workload is very light.

I hurry directly to the dairy, hoping to catch Josiah cleaning out the delivery truck, but to my dismay the truck is not back yet, which is odd since it's nearly four. I stand there a moment, wondering what to do. I'm about to turn around when I see Miriam emerging from the dairy. She spies me and waves eagerly, so I go over to speak to her. At the least it seems I should explain that I've moved — or rather that I've been moved.

"Rachel," she says a bit breathlessly. "Am I glad to see you."

"Hello, Miriam." I force a smile. "I just wanted to tell — "

"Have you heard the news? About Josiah?" Her eyes are glittering with what seems like alarm.

I take in a fast breath. "What's wrong? Is he okay? Was there a wreck?"

She waves her hand. "No, nothing like that."

"Well, what then?" I feel my impatience rising.

"Josiah ran off with Monique."

"What?" It feels like the earth is giving way beneath my feet. Her nod seems a bit too cheerful, almost as if she enjoys sharing this bad news. "It seems they were spotted leaving together early this morning. It was the same time Josiah always leaves to make his deliveries. But she was with him. And then Josiah ditched the delivery truck and took off with Monique — to God only knows where."

She shakes her head. "I knew that girl was no good from the start. She could hide those hideous tattoos beneath her dresses, but she couldn't hide the blackness of her heart." Now Miriam looks slightly apologetic. "I'm sorry, dear. I know you and Josiah were . . . well, you were good friends."

I don't know what to say and am trying to fight back tears.

"Reverend Jim is just brokenhearted about the whole thing. Poor man, he's treated Josiah like his own son. And now for him to go and do this? Well, it's just a shame." She shakes her finger in my face. "Remember what I told you about men and their predisposition to sinful ways? See why there are so many more good women than men?"

I want to deny this—to shout at her that Josiah is different, that he wouldn't do something like this—but how can I?

"I have to go." I'm about to leave but suddenly remember what I was going to tell her. "And I almost forgot. I've been relocated to—"

"I know all about that, Rachel." She smiles. "Congratulations."

"Congratulations?"

Miriam looks surprised. "To be invited to live in the prophet's house—surely, you know what an honor that is. I hope you'll work hard to prove you're worthy of it."

I can't even think of a response to that. Instead I just wave and turn away, jogging back toward the dining hall, where Eleanor looks slightly surprised to see me until I explain that I'm on my way to the garden. Then she turns back to her mixer, shaking her head.

It's not until I'm in the garden that tears begin to tumble again. I cannot believe Josiah has abandoned me like this. And with Monique? It's more than I can handle.

"What's wrong?" Hannah asks me with concerned eyes.

"I'm sorry." I use my sleeve to wipe my tears. "I'm just, uh, a little upset."

"I heard the news."

"Which news?" I ask eagerly, hoping she might know more than Miriam.

"That you're cooking for the reverend's family now."

"Oh . . . yeah." I tell her why I'm here and what I need. "But we need to hurry."

She leads me around, helping me to harvest the items on my list. As usual, she chats with me, explaining things about gardening and what's coming in good and the challenges she faces. Then, finally, just as we're picking tomatoes, I put my hand on her arm. "Can I ask you something?"

She looks surprised but stands up straight, slipping her shears into the little gardening apron she wears. "Sure. What?"

"Why did you come here?"

Now she looks worried, glancing over her shoulder.

"I mean, you seem different," I say quickly. "And I know you came by choice. But why?"

"You came by choice too," she points out.

"Kind of, but Josiah had a lot to do with it."

She sighs. "You're lucky to have him."

"But I don't have him." I hear how strained my voice sounds. "He's gone and I'm stuck here."

"I didn't know."

"It's a new development." Now I regret opening up to Hannah like this.

"Look. Some of us left really horrible lives behind. Compared to how I was living, this place is heaven."

"Really?" I find this hard to believe.

"My parents were messed up." She leans over and picks another tomato, then sets it on top of my basket. "Both of them were heroin addicts. I left home when I was sixteen. I thought I could make it on my own, but I got pulled into human trafficking." She sighs. "That's a story I'd rather not tell . . . and trust me, you don't want to hear it."

"I'm sorry."

"And now I get to do this." Hannah waves her arms to the greenery around her with a half smile. "Why should I complain?"

"What if you have to become someone's wife? What if one of the deacons decides to add you to his—his family?"

She shrugs. "There are worse things."

I look directly into her eyes. "I don't know about your previous life. It sounds sad. But does that mean you have to settle for this?" I look around the garden. "I don't mean this garden. It's beautiful. But you could have a garden out there, in the real world, and you could have a different sort of life."

She just shakes her head. "You say that, Rachel . . . but you're still here."

I hold up a defiant fist. "I'm here now. But I'm leaving."

"That's easier said than done."

"What do you mean?"

"I've said more than enough." She starts to walk away.

"Wait," I say as I go to catch her. "I feel like I can trust you, Hannah. What are you saying? Do they hold people here against their will?"

She gives me a blank look.

"Hannah?"

"I'll say this, Rachel. Be careful. If you really want out of here, don't tell anyone. Or else it will only get worse." She gives me a stern look. "I don't want to talk to you about this again. Do you understand?"

I just nod, then turn away. But as I walk back with my heavy basket of produce over my arm, I wonder at her words. It sounded like a serious warning. Like I can't just announce I'm ready to go and expect to leave. More than ever, I long for Josiah. I want to question him about this. I want him to help me get out of here.

For the first time since coming here, I feel myself praying in earnest. I'm no longer playing a religious game. Whether it's fear or desperation, I'm speaking directly to God in my heart. I'm pleading with him to help me. And as I pray this way, I realize that I no longer care to perform my way into God's favor. I'm simply telling him that I'm in trouble — serious trouble — and I need help.

I probably don't deserve God's help. And I'm well aware that I've made some stupid choices. I just hope the things I learned in church, things I learned long ago, about forgiveness and mercy — I hope these things are true. I hope that God won't forsake me. Because, more than ever, I need him now.

Keeping Hannah's warning in mind, I go right to work fixing dinner for Reverend Jim's oversized family. I act perfectly normal and try to make this a truly good meal. I don't want anyone to suspect I'm not perfectly happy with my new job. But the whole time I'm chopping and broiling and steaming and stirring, I'm concocting a plan — a way to get out of here. And I'm praying that God will help me.

After dinner, I take my sweet time in the kitchen. It's really Kellie's job to clean up, but I pretend to be doing some organizational tasks. I peruse the cookbooks and pretend to be obsessed with menu planning. And finally I start arranging things, getting it all set for breakfast in the morning.

"You really take your cooking seriously, don't you?" Kellie says as she closes the dishwasher and turns it on.

I force a smile. "Sure. I love cooking. Why shouldn't I?"

"Well, I think I'm done. Unless there's something else you need." I can tell by her expression she hopes I don't.

"No, that's great, Kellie. I just have a couple more things to finish up."

"Then you'll turn out the lights."

"Sure. Good night."

She seems a little unsure about leaving me alone, but she's also tired. I turn back to the cookbook that's still open, writing something down on the list I've been making. When I look up, she's gone. I putter around the kitchen for a while, making sure she's not coming back. And then, seeing that it's dusky outside, I turn off the kitchen lights, then go over to the back kitchen door. I slipped a piece of cardboard into this door earlier, in order to keep it unlocked and just slightly ajar, which convinces me that it's not connected to the security system.

My plan is to slip out there and climb over the wall. I studied it while working in the kitchen today, and I'm sure that it can't be any harder than the climbing wall my dad used to take me to on weekends. I feel certain I can make my way over it. I just hope I can safely make it down the other side. I plan to cut through the pasture and walk to the road, where I will hitchhike or, if necessary, walk back to the resort. Even if it's midnight, I'll call my mom—I'll tell her the truth and beg her to come and get me. This plan seems entirely doable to me.

Taking in a deep, steadying breath, I silently open the door and step out into the yard, but I'm barely out there when I hear the deep, sharp barking of a dog—or dogs—and immediately a pair of German shepherds charges at me. I leap back into the kitchen and slam the door against their lunging bodies.

With pounding heart, I stumble through the darkened kitchen and am about to duck out the door that leads to the north wing and my room when a man's voice tells me to "Stop!"

I turn just as the lights go on and am shocked to see Reverend Jim wearing only a pair of plaid pajama pants and holding a gun. "Oh, it's you," he says with relief. But then he frowns. "What were you doing in the backyard?"

I squint in the light. "I just wanted to go out for some fresh air."

"Really?" He looks skeptical.

"I always enjoy being out in the night air after a long day of being cooped up in the kitchen," I say quickly. At least this is true. "I had no idea there were guard dogs out there. I simply wanted to go sit outside and enjoy the stars and the sky."

Now he smiles. "Well, no reason you can't do that."

"Really?"

"Wait here." He points to the door. "I'll go put the dogs back in the kennel."

As I return to the door, I spot the piece of cardboard I'd used to stick in the door. I pick it up and tuck it in my pocket. Before long the dogs are gone and Reverend Jim is opening the door. "Come on out," he tells me. "There's a nice three-quarter moon out."

I'm trying to think of a way to tell him that he doesn't have to stay out here with me, but he's already sitting down on one of the patio chairs, nodding to the one opposite it. "Come on, Rachel, sit down. I've been wanting to talk to you anyway. This is a great opportunity."

I sit primly down on the chair, clasping my hands in my lap and trying not to stare at his pale bare chest. Reverend Jim must be about as old as my dad, but he doesn't seem to be in as good of shape.

"That was an excellent dinner," he tells me. "I meant to come in and tell you."

"Thank you." I can feel my palms sweating.

"I was surprised you didn't join us at the table. Celeste said you weren't quite comfortable with that yet. I hope that will change soon. We do consider you as part of our family. You know that, don't you?" He smiles broadly and his teeth glisten in the moonlight.

I nod. "Yes. Celeste has been very welcoming. It's just there was a lot to do, and I was getting used to the kitchen. And I didn't have time to clean up. I'll try to do better."

"That's just one of the things I like about you, Rachel. You try so hard. You always seem to give 110 percent." He reaches over, places his hand on my shoulder, and gives it a squeeze. "I appreciate that and I'm truly pleased to have you as part of our family." He stands with his hand still on my shoulder.

"Thank you." I can feel my heart pounding now — in that warning "take flight or fight" sort of way. And yet I remain sitting. Partly because it feels like the hand on my shoulder is pinning me there and partly because my knees feel like gelatin.

"I don't think you've met Jan yet, but I can assure you that Celeste and Kellie are already quite fond of you." He moves around behind me, placing a hand on my other shoulder, and now he's gently massaging my shoulders and upper back. "And I am too, Rachel. You're a talented and exceptionally pretty girl. And I can tell you have a heart to serve God and your fellow man. The first time Josiah brought you to us, I could tell you were a very special girl. Someone I wanted to get to know better."

I feel slightly sick to my stomach now. Strange because I barely ate any dinner. But I think if I suddenly threw up, it would put a quick end to this awkward moment.

"I can feel the tension in your shoulders," he calmly tells me as he continues to gently massage. "I'm sure it must be hard work cooking for all of us. You should try to relax more, Rachel. Work is good, but it's important to have fun too."

I swallow hard and somehow find the strength to stand up and turn around and face him. "You're right," I say in a raspy voice. "I am tired. It's been a long day."

He nods with a twinkle in his eye. Like he's enjoying some private joke. "I don't suppose you've heard the news."

"News?" I inch back toward the kitchen door.

"Josiah has left us." He holds up his hands with a sad expression.

I pretend to be shocked. "What do you mean?"

"Josiah decided that he doesn't fit in here."

"Why?"

"I'm not sure. All he said was that he'd had enough. He wanted to leave and never come back."

"Never?" My voice cracks and I'm on the verge of tears again. Not just because of Josiah running off, but also because of what I feel are the reverend's improper advances. And I do not think I'm imagining things.

"I'm sorry." He steps closer to me. "I know how you felt about Josiah." Again he places his hands on my shoulders. "But I do think it's for the best, Rachel. You belong here, but he does not." He lets out a sad sigh. "I had such hopes for him . . . for both of you. But Josiah has let me down." Now he pulls me close to him, enclosing me in a firm hug, and my face is pressed against his chest and the smell of him makes me feel truly ill. And I'm crying.

"Don't despair, my little one," he whispers in my ear. "I will take care of you."

Everything in me wants to scream and run. But the thought of that shiny gun . . . the guard dogs . . . Hannah's warning— I know I need to be careful. "Thank you," I say quietly. "It's upsetting to hear that about Josiah." I gently extract myself from his arms. "And I just need to process everything."

He touches my cheek, looking down at me with sympathetic eyes. "I understand, Rachel. Just remember you're in good hands now. You're with family. We'll take care of you."

"Thanks," I mutter. Then somehow I get away from him and into the house. I'm up in my room, my back leaning against the door as I try to catch my breath. I'm about to lock the door when I realize there is no lock. So I slide the big, long dresser in front of it. With my dress on, I climb into bed, and with tears of desperation sliding down my cheeks, I attempt to pray. But instead of truly praying, my mind is running in circles.

First I'm trying to figure out how Josiah could've left me like this. Then I'm trying to figure out how I'll get out of here. Like a ping-pong ball, I bounce back and forth between these two subjects. Finally I realize I'll never figure out why Josiah did this. Maybe someday my heart will heal. In the meantime, I need to devise a plan to escape from this place.

CHAPTER 17

After my second nearly sleepless night, I'm feeling both frazzled and fearful. As I make breakfast—which is only for four, the reverend and two of his wives and me—it takes all my concentration to stay focused on the food. I wish I could eat in the kitchen by myself, but Celeste has made it clear that I'm to join them.

And although they praise the crepes with berries and the eggs I scrambled with fresh veggies and cheese, I can only nod in a humble way as I try to look like I'm eating. But the food tastes like cardboard and sawdust, and my stomach is tied in knots. Even so, I force myself to shovel in some bites. I know I'll need the fuel if I'm going to pull off what I have in mind.

It isn't until after lunch that I attempt to convince Celeste that I need to get some more veggies for dinner. For some reason she doesn't seem to completely trust me. Perhaps I'm acting overly eager. "I suppose you could send Kellie," I tell her, trying to appear as if I don't really care. "But if the veggies are tough or not right, we can't really blame her. Selecting good produce is an acquired skill."

Celeste seems to get this. "I'm sure you're right. I've never been good at picking out melons or tomatoes."

"I could teach you."

Now she laughs, waving her hand dismissively. "No thank you. I'd rather delegate that responsibility to you. So be on your way then, Rachel. And while you're there, why don't you get some more of those delectable berries you served for breakfast. They were absolutely gorgeous."

"I'll do that." I reach for the basket, looping it over my arm. And just like that, I walk out of the house. Feeling like I've just been sprung from prison, I try not to look too eager or excited as I walk toward the dining hall and garden. I planned this all out last night. I will actually go to the garden as I said. And I will gather some vegetables and fruit. But instead of returning back through the dining hall, I will pretend to be interested in looking at the chickens even though I've been in the chicken yard before. I know there's a gate back there because I've seen Hannah pushing a wheelbarrow through it. My plan is to use it as my exit.

And because the chicken yard backs up to the woods, I suspect I can continue directly through the woods until I reach the creek trail, which I will follow on down to the footbridge. Then I'll take the secret path that leads to the hobbit hut Josiah built. There I will hide out until the sun sets. I'll use the light of the moon to find my way back over the footbridge and through the woods until I reach the cow pasture. I'll cut through the pasture until I reach the road. It seems like a good plan. By tonight, I'll be free.

I look down at my dress as I walk up to the dining hall. I specifically chose this one because the calico is dark with shades of purple and gray and black, and I hope it will be like camouflage and hide me as I make my getaway. I'm also wearing my sturdiest shoes.

I greet the kitchen workers and am relieved to see that Eleanor isn't there right now. That is a lucky break. She might notice that I don't pass back through the kitchen and get suspicious. My next lucky break is that Hannah is preoccupied with harvesting cucumbers that Eleanor wants for pickle making. I simply wave to her and tell her I'll help myself.

To keep this realistic as well as to have something to eat later, I do pick some produce. But I do this as quickly as I can without drawing attention to myself. Then I slip into the chicken yard and pretend to greet the chickens like I've seen Hannah do. I make my way across, open the gate, and hurry on my way.

My heart is pounding with anxiety as I press through the woods. If I take a straight course, I should reach the creek trail in about five minutes. However, it seems to take longer. When I finally reach the trail, I turn to go downstream, hurrying along, eager to reach my hideaway. My heart isn't pounding quite so furiously now, but I won't be able to breathe easily until I'm hidden safely within the hut.

Spying the footbridge, I begin to jog, eager to make it across — and then I see them. Two men are coming directly toward me. I stop in my tracks, tempted to turn and run the opposite direction. But then I hear the sound of barking. The men have a pair of large dogs on leashes. Probably Reverend Jim's guard dogs.

"Wait right there!" one of the men yells at me.

I remain still, desperately trying to concoct a story about why I'm out here like this as they hurry toward me with the dogs lunging on their leashes.

"What are you doing out here?" Deacon Clarence demands.

"I, uh, I came out to collect mushrooms."

"Mushrooms?" He narrows his eyes, and I suddenly remember how Monique ran away because this overweight middle-aged lecher wanted to marry her. "What mushrooms?" he growls at me.

"Wild mushrooms . . . in the woods," I say innocently. "I want to gather some for dinner tonight."

"What sort of mushrooms does one find in this part of Idaho?" Deacon Don speaks in a calmer tone. I know he's Bethany and Lydia's father. And for some reason he seems more sympathetic.

"Chanterelles."

Now he frowns. "You've seen them?"

"Oh yes," I assure him.

"Where are these chanterelles?"

I point across the creek. "Over there."

"Would you care to show us?"

"Don," Deacon Clarence says with irritation. "Can't you see she's lying?"

Don gives him a look. "Why don't we let her show us the *chanterelles*." He points at me. "Lead the way."

As I'm walking toward the footbridge, I can hear them whispering something behind me and then they start laughing.

"Let's not go on a wild-goose chase," Deacon Clarence calls out as I'm about to step on the bridge. "Deacon Don just told me he grew up in Oregon where chanterelles actually do grow. But he says they don't show up until autumn."

I turn to look at them.

"Sorry, Rachel." Deacon Don shakes his head. "But it was your own lie that trapped you."

"You're coming with us," Deacon Clarence sternly tells me.

There's no point to fight them. They have the power . . . and the dogs. Before long I'm sitting in the reverend's office, and he is looking at me with disappointment. "I was afraid it would come to this," he sadly tells me. "After Josiah left . . . I was worried you'd try to leave too."

I'm trying to think of something to say, but my brain feels fuzzy.

"You could fit in so well here, Rachel. You have all the qualities I look for in a young woman." He peers intently at me. "Are you truly that unhappy here?"

I nod, tears burning in my eyes. "I want to leave," I say meekly. "I wouldn't have tried to run away . . . except I didn't think you'd let me go."

"Do you think we hold people here against their will?"

I shrug. "I'm not sure. I guess I don't really know."

"I only want to care for my children. God has chosen me to guide and direct, to provide for and protect, to lead and teach. I try to do what I think is best for my children. But sometimes children rebel and go astray . . . sometimes children require loving discipline to help them get back on the right path."

Suddenly I remember something. "I'm only seventeen," I blurt out.

He only seems mildly surprised as he simply nods.

"To keep me here against my will is like kidnapping."

"Those are the laws of a flawed and sinful world. We have a higher law here."

"But I want to go."

"Enough!" He slams the palm of his hand on his desk, making a loud bang that makes me jump. Then he picks up the phone. "Send the deacons back in," he says in a flat tone.

And now Deacon Don and Deacon Clarence come in.

"Take her," the reverend tells them. He nods to Deacon Clarence. "I no longer have any use for her. But perhaps you can help bring her back to her senses."

"Come on, to your feet." Deacon Clarence roughly grabs me by the arm. And now the two of them—one on either side of me—are escorting me out of the reverend's office.

"You're hurting me." Then I remember being told that the best way to prevent being abducted is to make noise. "Please, don't do this!" I cry as they push me down the hallway. "I'm only seventeen. This is kidnapping. It's a criminal offense." Even as I scream for help, the men drag me through the reception area. Rose doesn't even look up from her desk.

"Rose! *Help me!* Call 911!"

Deacon Clarence laughs in a mean way. "She thinks that phone is an outside line." Then as we go outside, he shakes me. "Straighten up, girl!"

"This will be easier if you cooperate," Deacon Don warns me.

My mind is racing now. Somehow I have to make enough fuss and enough noise that someone will come out here to help me. But when I start to scream, Deacon Clarence smacks me with his closed fist. Not in the face, but against the side of my head and so hard that my ears are ringing and I think I see stars.

And then it all goes black.

. . . .

When I come to, I'm sitting on a hard cement floor in a tiny windowless room. There is a stained bare mattress in the corner and a bare lightbulb fixture on the ceiling above. But there's no light switch. Nothing else. The gray paint on the metal door is chipped and scuffed. And there is no doorknob. I stand, running my hand over the gray wall. It's made of cement.

This is not a room; it's a prison cell.

I begin to pace, back and forth . . . back and forth — the room is four steps across. My heart is racing with fear and my mind is spinning in circles as I try to figure out a plan. But I realize I cannot think my way out of this. Feeling desperate and hopeless, I sit on the nasty-looking mattress and cry.

But when I run out of tears, I just sit there, staring at the ugly gray walls, trying to make sense of what truly seems senseless. Finally, all I can think is that I am such a fool. Such a complete and utter fool. I deserve to be locked up like this. I brought this mess on myself with my own stupid naïveté and gullibility. I asked for this!

I am such a fool!

Eventually, I tire of berating myself. Yes, I am a fool. There's no disputing this fact. However, it does no good to wallow in it. Suddenly one thing is clear — crystal clear: Only God can get me out of this mess.

"Dear God," I pray aloud, unconcerned that anyone will hear me through these solid cement walls. Even if they can hear me, I don't really care. "Please, God, forgive me for making such a mess of my life. Forgive me for telling lies." I begin to list every time I deceived someone, starting with Josiah and my mom and even the people I lied to here, including Miriam and Eleanor and the nasty men who caught me today.

"I know they're wrong to do this to me. And I know they've lied and tricked me too. But maybe I asked for it by lying to them first." I go on and on, confessing everything I can think of and asking God to forgive me.

When I can't think of one more thing, I just sit in silence. I feel a tiny bit better, but it still looks hopeless. What time is it? I feel thirsty. Are they going to just leave me here until I die?

Feeling more and more thirsty, I wonder how long it takes to dehydrate and die of thirst. Probably a few days. Even so, all I can think is that I want a glass of water. And somehow this reminds me of a Bible story I heard in church before. The story about the woman who went to the well for water and was met by Jesus. He told her that he could give her living water . . . so she would thirst no more.

"Dear God, I think that's part of my problem . . . part of the reason I was attracted to this place—I mean, besides being attracted to Josiah. But I think I came here and stayed here because I was spiritually thirsty. Not for Reverend Jim's messed-up teaching and doctrine. I mean *Jim* because that man is no reverend. Jim Davis is a wolf in sheep's clothing. A trickster. I know this now." I get back on my feet, pacing back and forth again, trying to firmly grasp the truth that's washing through me like living water.

"I was thirsty for you, God. I wanted your truth." Even as I say the word *truth*, I remember something from my old church days. *You'll know the truth, and the truth will set you free.* Those words rush through my heart and my head, as fresh and clean as living water. I say the words aloud: "I'll know the truth, and the truth will set me free."

And just like that, I know—God's word is the truth.

I start to replay all the Bible stories I can remember from the years spent at church. I recall the story Jesus told about the two men who built houses by the sea—one on the sand and one on the rock. And I know Jesus is the rock. I know that's who I want to build my life on. I remember other things Jesus said, like how he is the way and the truth and the life and that no one comes to the father unless they come through him. Not Jim Davis.

I don't know how long I go through all these things, but my thirst for water is no longer troubling me. And I get the feeling that I'm going to be okay. No matter how this turns out, God is with me now. I can feel his presence like I've never felt it before. I am truly experiencing the peace that passes understanding. I remember hearing people talk about this in my old church, but it never felt real before. Now it's right here and it's real.

I jump when I hear the door being unlocked and opened. And my heart pounds as I brace myself for whatever is going to happen next. I'm relieved to see it's a woman and she has a bowl and a cup in her hands.

"Don't try anything," she warns me. "Deacon Clarence is out in the hallway, and he'll deal with you if you try to get away."

I look evenly at her. "I'm not going to try anything. But I do know that God is with me."

She looks surprised.

"And I know the truth now. And the truth will set me free."

She places the bowl and cup on the floor, backing toward the partially opened door. "Well, don't expect anyone to set you free from here."

"I'm already free," I calmly tell her. "God's truth is inside of me now — just like real living water. And from now on I'm building my life on Jesus' words and teaching." I point at her. "You should do the same. Because I'm warning you, Jim Davis is a wolf in sheep's clothing and he'll — "

"Shut up!" she yells, waving her hands at me. "Get thee behind me, devil!" Then she hurries out and slams the door, and the sound of the dead bolt sliding into place echoes in the room.

"Who's in prison now?" I say quietly. But she can't hear me. I go over to see what's in the bowl and cup. The cup looks like water and the bowl contains some murky-looking brown soup.

I give it a sniff, wondering if they might poison me, but it smells like beef and vegetables.

I take a cautious sip and it seems okay. Even so, I pray over my meal, asking God to bless it. I slowly eat the lukewarm soup, and I'm tempted to save the water until later. But she might return for the dishes and take the water. So I drink it down.

Then I begin to pace again. But this time, instead of fretting and worrying about my desperate situation, I continue trying to recall everything I can remember from my church days. I even sing some songs that make me feel better.

It's funny because I used to think I never learned anything at that church. And I used to blame the church split for my problems. I think I even used it as my excuse to push God out of my life. But now I realize I learned a lot of good stuff at that church. They really did believe in the Bible. Sure, they had problems and disagreements. But who doesn't? At least they were trying to build their house on the rock.

I'm guessing about an hour has passed before I hear the door opening again. This time a different woman comes in. She's much younger, but there's a hardness to her as she sets a dirty plastic bucket down, then picks up the bowl and cup.

"What's that?" I ask her.

She gives me a disgusted look. "It's your *restroom*."

"Oh. How long are they going to keep me here?" I ask as she's reaching for the door.

She scowls at me. "How long will it take you to come to your senses?"

I actually smile at her. "I'm already at my senses."

Now she looks curious. "Really?"

"God is with me in here. He's showing me how his truth will

set me free. I can see now that Jim Davis is a wolf in sheep's clothing and anyone who believes him is—"

"Shut up, you stupid sinful girl! That kind of talk will never get you out of here." She steps out. "You deserve this."

Once again the door slams, but this time the light goes out. I blink in the pitch-black darkness, trying to see, but it's useless. I've never seen such darkness. I slide my feet across the floor until I feel the edge of the mattress. Then I ease myself onto it and lie down.

For some reason—probably the darkness—I feel afraid again. But instead of giving in to it, I try to recall the words to Psalm 23. When I was in sixth grade, our whole Sunday school class memorized the shepherd's psalm from the Bible. It takes me a while to really get it word for word. Then I go over it a few more times. Finally I think I got it. And I find real comfort in the words:

> The LORD is my shepherd, I lack nothing.
>> He makes me lie down in green pastures,
> he leads me beside quiet waters,
>> he refreshes my soul.
> He guides me along the right paths
>> for his name's sake.
> Even though I walk
>> through the darkest valley,
> I will fear no evil,
>> for you are with me;
> your rod and your staff,
>> they comfort me.
>
> You prepare a table before me
>> in the presence of my enemies.

You anoint my head with oil;
  my cup overflows.
Surely your goodness and love will follow me
  all the days of my life,
and I will dwell in the house of the LORD
  forever.

As best I can tell, this is my third day in solitary confinement. And although I've had dark moments of frantic fear and hopeless desperation, I try not to surrender to them. Instead I talk to God, telling him exactly how I'm feeling. And then I sing songs and replay all the scriptures and parables I can remember from my church days.

Sometimes, like when they turn out the lights, I compare myself to Jonah in the whale. As I recall, Jonah didn't want to obey God either—that's what got him into his mess. But eventually God rescued him. I believe God is going to rescue me too. Just the same, I contrived a way to keep track of how many days I've been here by poking holes in this disgusting mattress. Three holes equals three days.

Although I get "three meals" a day, they are frugal at best. My stomach is constantly rumbling, and I wonder how long a person can survive on runny oatmeal with no milk (which seems crazy since this place has a dairy), two bowls of watery soup, and three cups of water.

The upside is that I've only had to use my bucket toilet twice since I came here. The downside is that I don't feel too well. The young woman is the only one delivering meals and picking up my toilet bucket now.

But each time I see her, I try to be polite and cordial. I know now that she's about to become Clarence's new wife. And part of me should be relieved because one of my concerns when I discovered that my "secure room" was in Clarence's house was that he was considering me for part of his harem. But for this girl's sake, I feel sorry. I try to be nicer to her. And I finally discover her name is Glory and she's a deacon's daughter.

By my "dinnertime" on the third day, Glory seems a tiny bit friendlier. Or else she's just bored. "You know Deacon Clarence would let you out of here if you'd just repent and apologize," she tells me as she lingers by the food. "I heard that Reverend Jim still thinks there's hope for you . . . if you can straighten up." She tips her head to one side. "Can't you just repent and say you're sorry?"

"I've already done that. To God."

She seems to consider this. "Do you want me to tell them that?"

I shrug. "I don't care." I study her closely. "How old are you anyway?"

She folds her hands across her front with a stubborn look. "None of your business."

"Sorry." I sigh. "I just thought you might be around my age."

"How old are you?"

"Seventeen."

I can tell by her eyes that she must be the same age, unless she's younger.

"And as much as I felt I loved Josiah, I wouldn't even have wanted to marry him at my age."

Now she looks really interested. "Why not? Josiah seemed like a great guy. Well, except that he strayed."

"I just think seventeen is way too young to get married. There are so many things I want to do with my life before I tie myself down like that."

I can tell I hit a nerve as she steps closer to the door. "It's a great honor to be chosen as a deacon's wife."

"Is it what you want?"

Her gaze darts about, almost as if she's worried someone could be listening.

"How many years have you lived here?" I ask. "Most of your life?"

Now she looks angry, reminding me of how she was when I first met her. "Quit asking me so many questions, Rachel. You're the one who should be questioned. Ask yourself how long you think you can live in here like this. Because until you change, you won't be getting out." She lowers her voice. "And it could get worse."

"Worse?"

She steps behind the door. "Repent," she says loudly. "Turn from your sinful ways." Then she slams the door and the lights go out.

This is a new trick. Usually the lights don't go out until she picks up my dishes from dinner. My stomach growls hungrily, and I carefully crawl on my hands and knees to the corner where the dishes are placed. Feeling cautiously with my fingers, lest I accidentally spill them, I finally feel the edge of the bowl. And without using the spoon, I simply drink it. I can taste chicken broth and some mushy vegetables.

Then I feel around until I reach the water, drinking it as well. Finally I crawl back to the mattress, and after I lie down, I quietly sing old praise songs, ones I learned in church, as many as I can remember . . . until I fall asleep.

· · · · · · · · · ·

I have no idea what time it is when I wake up. As usual, I'm surprised at the thick black darkness all around me. I blink and blink, thinking my eyelids have been glued shut. But then I remember where I am, and I feel like sobbing and crying and pounding my fist into this smelly mattress. But instead I pray.

"Please, God," I cry out. "Please, please help me. I know you'll give me the strength I need to endure this. You've been giving me strength all along. But I'm starting to wear out. My stomach hurts. I feel weak. Please, God, please help me to get out of here. *Please.*"

I want to be stronger. I want to have more faith. But I feel beaten here in the darkness. And now I'm sobbing again as my faith is being shaken to the core. Finally, the only thing I can do is to recite the shepherd's psalm. I say it over and over, again and again and again. Eventually I just keep repeating these lines: "Even though I walk through the darkest valley, I will fear no evil, for you are with me . . ."

The next time I wake up, it's still dark, yet somehow I know it's daytime out there. But no one comes to turn on the light. No one brings me my watery oatmeal. I just sit here, trying not to be afraid. Once again, I go through all I can remember of Bible verses. I sing songs. And mostly I pray. But it feels like hours have gone by and I think I've been forgotten completely. Like they have truly locked me up and thrown away the key.

I'm tempted to pound on the door and scream for help, but I might get more attention from them by remaining silent. Maybe they will think I've died and send someone in to carry me away. In fact, this gives me an idea. What if I lie down and act like I'm deathly ill? Would that be enough for them to take me out of here?

As much as I'm thirsting for water right now, I'm also thirsting for light. And then I remember those are two of the things that Jesus promised. "You are the light of the world," I say quietly. "You are my living water," I say this over and over and am surprised at how comforting it is.

Suddenly the light comes on, and shielding my eyes from the blinding glare, I sit up, completely forgetting my earlier plan to play possum.

"Rachel!" a woman's voice cries.

Blinking into the brightness, I squint to see a woman — who looks like my mom — lunging toward me. She takes me in her arms, holding me and rocking me like a small child. "Oh, Rachel, Rachel. Are you all right?"

"Mom?" My voice comes out raspy as I peer at her. "Is it really you?"

"Get her out of here," says a man's voice.

I peer up to see a strange man standing behind her.

"What's happening?" I ask, confused.

"Come on," Mom urges, helping me to my feet. "We're leaving. Now."

"But how?" I ask as she leads me out. "Won't they stop us?"

"No one is going to stop you," the man says.

"That's Detective Harris," Mom tells me as she leads me down a long hallway and up some dimly lit stairs. "Josiah helped us."

"Josiah?"

We're inside of what looks like a normal kitchen now, and I remember that I was in Clarence's house. But it all feels strange and dreamlike. "Is this real?"

Mom's arm is wrapped around my shoulders as she leads me. "It all seems pretty surreal to me," she says quietly.

We go past a room where uniformed policemen appear to be holding members of this household. I recognize several faces, including Glory's. I pause, pointing into the room. "That girl," I urgently tell the detective beside me. "Glory. She's underage, and they're going to force her to marry Clarence."

The detective nods. "We'll get to the bottom of this later, Rachel. Let's get you outside now."

There are several black-and-white police cars out there as well as some dark-colored cars. My mom and the detective lead me to a slate-colored sedan with tinted windows, and we slide into the backseat. To my surprise, Josiah is sitting in the front passenger side. The detective gets into the driver seat, and to my relief, the car begins moving.

"Are you all right?" Josiah asks with what seems like genuine concern.

"I—uh—I think so."

My mom reaches into a bag by her feet and hands me a bottle of water. I eagerly take a sip. I think I'm in shock, trying to absorb all of this. My mom? Josiah? The police? "How did this happen?"

"That's what we want to know," Detective Harris says as he drives past the dairy barn. "I have lots of questions. But first we'll take you to the clinic at the resort to make sure you're okay."

Mom is still holding me close to her. Almost as if I'm five years old again. I look at her, studying her face and trying to grasp what's happening. But she looks nearly as confused as I feel. "How did you do this?" I ask her. "How did you know where to find me?"

She nods to Josiah, who is turned around in the seat, peering at me. "You should ask him."

"But he abandoned me," I say in a hurt tone.

"No, I did not." He frowns.

"You and Monique," I say. "You ditched me here and—"

"That's not how it happened."

"Let him tell you," Mom says gently.

I take another sip of water and wait.

"I was leaving the grounds, just like usual, to do my deliveries," he begins. "But before I got to the gates, I saw Monique walking along. I remembered what you said about her wanting to get away before they forced her to marry Clarence. So I stopped and picked her up, planning to drop her off at the bus stop in town. But before I got there, a patrol car pulled me over. I was accused of stealing my uncle's truck, which is ridiculous. But I had to go to jail anyway."

"He called Nadine from the jail," Mom tells me.

"Nadine?" I try to imagine this. "To bail you out?"

"No. I called her to get help for you," he explains. "I was worried about you, Rachel."

"For good reason," Mom says.

"Unfortunately, Nadine didn't buy my story at first," Josiah tells me. "She couldn't believe that Lost Springs Dairy was such a diabolical sort of place."

"But a couple days later Nadine called me," Mom says. "Apparently she did her own research and decided that Josiah's warning was legit. Of course, I was skeptical when she told me all this. It sounded so far-fetched and crazy. Besides, as I told Nadine, you were too sensible to get pulled into something like that."

"I'm not as sensible as you think," I mutter.

"You were deceived," Josiah says. "By my uncle. I was deceived too. And so are the others. I'll admit that I wanted to believe he was building something good. Even more so when you came to live there. But the more I found out, the worse it all felt to me. And every time I questioned my uncle, he got angry. The last straw was when he had me arrested. That was unbelievable. After he pressed charges, he came to the jail, warning me never to show my face at Lost Springs again. That's when I knew you were in serious trouble."

I just nod, but a chill runs down my spine to remember how it felt to be locked up like that. So helpless and alone.

"I'm so sorry I ever brought you here, Rachel. When I think what might've happened to you . . ." He grimly shakes his head.

"So how did you get out of jail?" I ask. I cannot miss the irony of how we were both locked up at the same time. Although being in jail sounds preferable to where I was being held.

"Nadine covered my bail to get me out," Josiah explains. "She even helped me to get a lawyer. And when the authorities heard my story, they were pretty interested."

"It took a couple of days to get the warrants in place," the detective says as he drives. "But we couldn't risk coming in here without having everything in order. Not if we wanted to make arrests and make them stick."

"I was so worried," Mom tells me. "I was staying with Nadine, but I called some of our old church friends and asked them to pray for you. Alice McIntire put you on a prayer chain."

"They have a prayer chain?"

"Yes. And they're having church services too. At a school. Alice got about fifty people praying for you, Rachel. They were praying 'round the clock."

"Wow." I let out a sigh. "I think I could feel it."

Mom squeezes me. "I'm so thankful you're okay." She peers curiously into my eyes. "You are okay, aren't you? They didn't hurt you . . . or anything?"

"I'm okay," I assure her as I take another sip. "Well, besides being hungry. But really, I'm better than okay."

"How is that possible?" she asks. "I saw where they were keeping you." She grimaces. "I've never seen anything so horrible. That place was disgusting. And being all alone in the darkness like that. I can't even imagine."

"But I wasn't alone," I say. "God was with me. He was my light in the darkness. He was my living water when I was thirsty."

The car is silent and Mom looks stunned.

"You're a strong girl, Rachel Hebert." Josiah smiles at me, and I can see the open admiration in his eyes.

"Thanks for helping me," I shyly tell him. "I mean, by calling Nadine and talking to the police." I feel unsure around him . . . wondering what our relationship will be or if we are finished. For all I know, he could be going back down under. "I honestly thought you'd abandoned me."

"I would never do that, Rachel."

"What will you do now?" I ask him. "Where will you go?"

"Nadine has offered him a job managing the ice cream shop," Mom tells me.

"Seriously?" I study Josiah's profile as he looks out at the cows grazing peacefully in the meadow. We're nearly to the security gates now. "Will you do that?"

"We'd sure appreciate it if he stuck around here awhile," the detective says. "Until we get this case wrapped up."

"What about me?" I ask. "Won't you need my help too?"

"You are going home with me," Mom declares.

"Yes," Josiah says in a protective way. "I think you'll be safer there."

"We'll take your deposition at the station," the detective informs me. "And we'll be in touch with you as needed regarding the upcoming trial. But Josiah and your mom are right, Rachel. You need to go home now."

I look into Josiah's eyes, knowing I will miss him.

"I'd like to stay in touch," he says quietly — as if reading my mind.

"Me too." I take another swig of water, amazed at how good it tastes.

Mom is holding my hand and gives it a gentle squeeze. "I can't believe all you endured, Rachel." She peers into my eyes as if searching for something. "You've been through so much. Are you sure you're okay?"

"I'm even better than okay. I know it probably doesn't make complete sense. And some might think an ordeal like that would make a person crazy. But I actually found the truth in that horrid prison cell. *God's real truth*. And even when I was still locked up, that truth really did set me free."

1. Rachel describes herself as an "old-fashioned" girl. On a scale of one to ten (1 = Laura Ingalls; 10 = Lady Gaga), how would you rank yourself? Explain why.

2. Why do you think Belinda and Lorna decided to frame Rachel in the missing-money scam at Nadine's? What could Rachel have done to handle that situation differently?

3. Do you think Rachel's crush on Josiah influenced her interest in attending his uncle's church? Have you ever been influenced by a crush? If so, describe.

4. What was your first impression of Lost Springs? If you'd been Rachel's friend, what would you have said to her about the place?

5. A lot of people were living at Lost Springs. What sort of things do you think had initially drawn them to it?

6. What would you describe as the most attractive part of Lost Springs? The least?

7. Rachel and Josiah felt they were spiritually tricked and deceived by Reverend Jim. Have you ever been deceived like that? Explain how that made you feel.

8. How would you define a cult church?

9. List five ingredients you believe contribute to a healthy church.
10. Do you know anyone who's involved in a cult church? If so, how does that make you feel? Is there anything you'd like to say to that person?
11. What kinds of safeguards are in your life to prevent you from ever being deceived like Rachel was?

MELODY CARLSON has written more than two hundred books for all age groups, but she particularly enjoys writing for teens. Perhaps this is because her own teen years remain so vivid in her memory. After claiming to be an atheist at the ripe old age of twelve, she later surrendered her heart to Jesus and has been following him ever since. Her hope and prayer for all her readers is that each one would be touched by God in a special way through her stories. For more information, please visit Melody's website at www.melodycarlson.com.

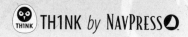

MY LIFE IS **TOUGHER** THAN MOST **PEOPLE REALIZE.**

I TRY TO KEEP EVERYTHING IN BALANCE: FRIENDS, FAMILY, WORK, SCHOOL, AND GOD.

IT'S NOT EASY.

I KNOW WHAT MY PARENTS BELIEVE AND WHAT MY PASTOR SAYS.

BUT IT'S NOT ABOUT THEM. IT'S ABOUT ME...

ISN'T IT TIME I OWN MY FAITH?

THROUGH THICK AND THIN, KEEP YOUR HEARTS AT ATTENTION, IN ADORATION BEFORE CHRIST, YOUR MASTER. BE READY TO SPEAK UP AND TELL ANYONE WHO ASKS WHY YOU'RE LIVING THE WAY YOU ARE, AND ALWAYS WITH THE UTMOST COURTESY. 1 PETER 3:15 (MSG)

www.navpress.com | 1-800-366-7788   TH1NK *by* NAVPRESS